All Hallows Eve

All Hallows Eve

Finally got around to publishing something! Enjoy! Mike

F.M. Stewart

Copyright © 2011 by F.M. Stewart.

ISBN: Softcover   978-1-4568-5306-8
        Ebook   978-1-4568-5307-5

All rights reserved. No part of this book may be reproduced or transmitted in any form or by any means, electronic or mechanical, including photocopying, recording, or by any information storage and retrieval system, without permission in writing from the copyright owner.

This is a work of fiction. Names, characters, places and incidents either are the product of the author's imagination or are used fictitiously, and any resemblance to any actual persons, living or dead, events, or locales is entirely coincidental.

This book was printed in the United States of America.

To order additional copies of this book, contact:
Xlibris Corporation
1-888-795-4274
www.Xlibris.com
Orders@Xlibris.com
92559

Evening One

The Little Princess of Snow Lake

Once upon a time, there lived a young princess in a land far, far away to the north. The winters were very cold. The land was covered with snow. The lakes and rivers froze. The king taught the princess to ice skate on a frozen lake outside the castle. Everyone in the kingdom liked to ice skate. The princess had silver skates and dressed in a silver dress. The king in his blue jerkin and his leather pants would skate for hours with his daughter and all the villagers. The queen would order the servants too take hot tea and cakes to all the skaters. From the castle balcony over looking the lake, the queen dressed in flowing white robes and would look down at the frozen lake. The king and princess skated for many happy hours. The queen shook her head in amazement at how much they loved to skate together. Then she would smile and have her lady in waiting bring her ice skates. The queen rushed out of the castle. Everyone in the castle and all the villagers would ice skate on the lake, creating a winter festival . . .

"Daddy, read it funny." The little girl interrupts. A man sits in a chair beside his daughter's bed with an open story book.

"What?"

"You know. Change the story and make it funny. So it's not boring."

"Okey dokey. Let me think a bit. Take a semi interesting fairy tale and make it fun for a little kid with a head cold. That's gonna be tough. I don't know if anyone's done that before. If they did they should have wrote a book or made a movie or something." He replies, stalling for time to think of ways to change the story. The book had pencil and pen marks, words scratched in the margins. The end of the story was completely crossed out and new lines written in. He begins to read.

Soon the festival became the highlight of the winter since no one had TV except for the king and queen. And so their subjects didn't have three different channels to watch every night. No Saturday morning cartoons. Why they didn't even have a public TV station so they could lie and say they watched public TV and not the network channels. The only thing the people in the kingdom had to watch was the little Princess as she skated. So the people in the kingdom, too poor to afford their own skates, would huddle together to watch the little ice princess do what skaters do. Apparently something called a Lutz and there's picking involved perhaps of noses or ticks because the huddled subjects were a dirty stinking lot that didn't bathe in the cold winter water.

People came from far and wide. Wherever far and wide is, perhaps a place of fat people from a long distance away, anyway they came to the kingdom during the winter festival. People sat for hours on carved ice benches as she whirled and twirled, ice sprayed from her skates like a magic dust bringing quiet contentment to the kingdom. Or so they said since people sat silent and still in their cold seats. But the people didn't move because their buttocks were frozen since they were sitting on blocks of ice.

One day, a sick little boy could not attend the festival because he froze his butt off from sitting on those ice benches. He requested an audience with the princess. The king and queen, thinking it would be good publicity, and might get them on the evening news, readily agreed. Unfortunately, the king and queen forgot they had no TV station and their subjects had no TVs. They ruled in a cold land, wintry year round so how smart could they be. Anyway, the interview went ahead and a TV station did cover the event. A public TV station, as the queen did lament.

The princess went to the boy's hovel of a house. He rose to greet her though he was in obvious distress. To present her with a shoe box he had clutched to his chest. The box was adorned with elaborately painted scenes. Most were of the young princess. Walking stiffly to her, thrusting out the box for her to take. Touched by his gift, a tear fell from his eye and onto his hand. Was it love at first sight? She took the box and opened it wide. Her nose was assaulted by a ferocious smell. The boy grinned and said, the fart gland is still attached as the contents of the box let out another whiney fart. Was this boy another Van Gogh? It was the boy's buttocks. It was his heinie, that was frozen off.

The princess was in shock. The reporter told the camera man to keep filming. Her eyes watery from the smell. The princess thrust the box back to the boy who then fell. Landing on the part of his anatomy where his butt used to be. At just that moment, the queen came through the open doorway as the boy's frozen heinie flew into the air. Like a pair of glasses, the buttocks landed on her face. Her nose nestled gently in the crack. The king came in next.

Seeing the scene: the boy with no butt, his queen wearing them as spectacles and his daughter weeping. All this on film and on the tube was too much. The king would be the 'butt' of jokes on all the TV talk shows watched by his fellow monarchs. I'm getting out of here the king declared. He promptly abdicated his throne and was on the next ship for Aruba.

"The end. Okay, time for bed, young lady." The man closes the story book he had been reading to his daughter. He had changed the story quite a bit. There were paragraphs that had been crossed out and notes scribbled in the margins and there were several places were his notes in pencil were erased and replaced with new sentences.

"More, more!" The little girl said, almost 7 years old.

"Been a big night for you. All that candy gave you a tummy ache. Hope your Mom doesn't find out how much I let you eat." He says grinning, looking around furtively for his wife.

"I wanted to do more trick or treating." The little girl pouted as she let out a loud sneeze.

"Here, hon, blow your nose." The man says as he hands her a tissue. "You can stay out longer next year when you don't have a cold. Hey, I did get you some chocolate. Better make sure I got all the wrappers." He looks around on the bed.

"Time to get some sleep." He rises from the bed side, tucks her blankets around her, kisses her on the head and slips toward the door and flips off the light switch and steps out into the hallway. He closes the door, leaving a small crack for light to peek into the bedroom.

He walks down the carpeted hallway, down two doorways and turns right into the next room, turns on the light and closes the door. The linoleum is cool on his bare feet as he lifts the toilet lid, drops his pants and sits down.

Just as he gets nestled in and grabs the sports page, there's a knock on the bathroom door.

"David?" His wife asks in a questioning tone of voice as if there could be someone else in their bathroom at this time of night. "David, you didn't put the storm windows on today and you go back to work tomorrow."

"I know, I ran out of time." He lies.

"Well, it needs to get done and you need to run the mower over the yard one more time before winter arrives." She reminds him. She opens the door a little to look in at him.

"Okay. Close the door. I'll do it next weekend for sure." He replies, his bowels rumble but no progress.

"David."

"Yea."

"We need to balance the checkbook and go over the benefits for your job, health and life insurance, pension."

"Really? I'm bushed. You know all about that stuff?"

"Now that you have a job at the plant, it's more than just a paycheck, there are other benefits we need to understand and use."

"Okay." He says. She closes the door and he hears the soft swish of her slippers she walks away. He thought getting this job would please Doris; she had been after him for months to get a job at the auto plant, particularly since they had a daughter. He was lucky to get the job; you had to know someone. Fortunately for David, the personnel manager had played high school football with his dad.

He makes a mental note to put the storm windows on, mow the yard, and put a lock on the bathroom door.

Evening Two

Chapter 1

It's Halloween, it's payday and David is sitting in a bar. Over the past year, this has become his regular payday habit after getting off work. One beer and joking around with other bar patrons before going home. On his usual stool, David is verbally sparring with Lenny, a regular customer in the bar. The challenge is to see who can tell the lamest jokes. The judges are whoever happens to be in the bar but the head judge is Wilbur, the owner and bartender. Wilbur is a retired steel worker, and a US Marine. He still has a buzz cut, his hair just grayer and thinner. Thicker around the waist but still solid, he and the lanky Lenny are veterans of the Korean War.

The bar is a slice of a place between two new buildings, a three story bank on one side and a two story Italian restaurant on the other side. This trio of buildings share parking in back and there are alley ways on the bank and restaurant side for people to walk around to the front door of Wilbur's bar. And with the bank closed for the day there is plenty of parking. There is a lot of new construction on this block. Two new buildings and a gas station were going in just up the street. A big pit was dug for the gas station's fuel storage tank.

The bank closes at 5:00 so the jukebox noise doesn't bother them and the restaurant has its own jukebox playing. Walking into the bar, a long wooden bar of indistinct dark wood runs the length of the room on the right with backless, circular seat barstools bolted to the floor. In the back were the bathrooms. On the left were five tables with four wooden chairs each. The tables and chairs were a little to close to make room on that side and in the back for a pool table. The cues and balls were behind the bar with Wilbur. Glazed windows in the front let in some light and several light fixtures illuminated the room well, more light than most bars. Probably because Wilbur wanted a bar for drinking and talking not hooking up.

Wilbur slides a mug of beer to David. "How's it hanging kid?"

"Low and lazy." David replies. Lenny is sitting next to him, already on his third beer.

"Okay, I got one." Lenny says, a cigarette dangling from his lip.

"Keep em clean tonight gentlemen." Wilbur warns them, nodding his head toward a young woman sitting at a table. Usually it's guys from the plant or bank tellers from next door, Wilbur assumed the lady worked for the bank although he doesn't recognize her, or people killing time before going to the restaurant which appears to be the case for the older couple sitting at a table next to the woman and another man at the table farthest in back. The man had been drinking double whiskey sours for the last two hours, one after the other. He didn't seem impaired so Wilbur kept serving him. The man was reading a newspaper though he had been looking up from his paper from time to time as if waiting for someone. When the woman had strolled in, the man had put the paper down and every now and then, with a cat-like grin, casually looked over at the woman. She had noticed the man and tried her best to not look his way. The man was about her age, later twenties, in jeans and a button-down blue shirt but no tie; he had blonde hair that was sandy and a bit ragged as if he was a couple of weeks overdue for a haircut. He was slim with a build more like David than Lenny although this man seemed to chain smoke as many cigarettes as Lenny. In the glance the woman had of the man, not that she thought he was unattractive but she didn't like the lines around his eyes or mouth that looked like he spent more time grimacing than smiling. She makes a conscious effort to look away and wished that the man wouldn't look over her way so much and go back to reading his paper.

"Okay, I still got one." Lenny clears his voice. "Did you hear about the eyeglass maker who got caught in his machine? He made a spectacle of himself!"

A collective groan erupts from the room.

"Since we're in a bar, how about this one?" David asks. "What do you call a cheerleader's favorite drink? Root beer!"

Another collective groan but not quite as loud.

Lenny throws out another. "What do you get if you cross and oyster and owl? A creature that dispenses pearls of wisdom."

"What kind of man never works a day in his life? A night watchman!" David counters.

"Hey that's my joke, I was going to say what kind of guy never works a day in his life? The answer: David!" Lenny laughs. "You got the sweetest set up, the uniform and badge and you hardly have to get your hands dirty."

David laughs too because it's true. He does have a nice job that uses his artistic talents and craftsman skills. The hours are demanding, sometimes he has to work late or go in at night to finish a project before the test personnel or some big shot from corporate comes breezing in. He doesn't work on the line; he is in the development department working with devices that deploy inflatable bags in a head on collision. He works with gold and other precious metals shaping contact points for the triggers for the bags in the steering column. That's why he has the identification card and uniform. Otherwise he couldn't get near the office because of the gold and platinum stored there. Lenny claps David on the back as they turn back to the bar for a sip of their beers.

"I think this guy is hilarious." A soft, feminine voice says from behind them as she lightly touches David on the shoulder.

Both David and Lenny stop in mid sip not because they were surprised at a women being in the bar, they assumed she worked at the bank next door, fraternization between the bank people and the factory people does happen occasionally, particularly after a couple of drinks. What did surprise them was that someone would describe their jokes as hilarious. They had been called lame, silly, and sort of funny and a local news anchor, who had mistakenly wandered into the bar and not the restaurant next door, had even said their jokes were mildly humorous.

They both turn in their stools. The young blonde woman is smiling at David with a little half smile that women learn in High School and men go to their graves yearning for any woman to flash that half smile at them. She has shoulder length hair, wore a mid thigh blue skirt and tight white blouse which probably pushed the boundary of the banks dress code. She wasn't skinny like a lot of the women David had seen in magazines and TV commercials but had a shape with curves in all the right places. David noticed that her front teeth were slightly bent inward toward each other, but didn't impact her attractiveness one bit.

"Hi, I just wanted to tell you that you're a funny guy." She had been seated at the table by the door. "I'm so glad I came in, it's such a friendly place, I mean you never know going into a neighborhood bar." She turns to Wilbur and mouths the words two more beers and turns back to David. "I'm Lena by the way." She reaches her hand out and David shakes her hand, she lingers over the handshake for a Moment.

"I'm David and this is Lenny." Lenny nods, knowing he is a third wheel in this conversation. He slides down a few stools as the woman hip checks her way next to David. He gets a whiff of her perfume as she sidles in beside him.

"Well, this evening is taking a turn for the better. I did have reservations next door, but my brother ~~local news anchor~~ never showed so now I have to wait but that's okay." She smiles at him.

"Well, I know the owner next door, I could . . ." David offers.

"You know I'm not so hungry anymore. I'll call my doofus brother and tell him off for standing me up. All of the sudden I'm thirsty. How about buying a girl a drink?"

"Uh, sure, I guess. I thought you just ordered . . ."

She looks at David for a Moment as if she had just met the dumbest guy in the world.

"Oh right. Well Sure I'd be happy to buy you a drink but you see the fact is, and it's not because I'm cheap, I'll buy you a drink, its just that I'm in that situation where you have a commitment with a women where you have a family in church kind of thing, kids and so on."

"You're married."

"Yes, that's it. Married. I'm married."

"I figured that out when I saw the ring you've been twisting on your finger. But I have a question though." She pauses, lightly licking her red lips.

"What's that?" David asks.

"Are you twisting it because you're nervous or so you can take it off?"

Realizing what he's doing he jerks his hands apart and hits his beer mug almost sending it over the other side of the bar.

The women laughs, leaning back on her bar stool. "Relax. David was it? I'm just flirting a bit. Tell you what; I'll buy you a martini. Want to sit over at my table?" She gestures to where she had been sitting. "Why don't you bring the beers over?" She turns and walks back over to her table, she glances at the man in the back who had been watching her. She quickly turns away from his direction when he tries to look her in the eyes.

David watches her walk away. Wilbur comes down the bar with the beers.

"Kid, none of my business, but I'm going to stick my nose in anyway, I don't like this. Doesn't it strike you as kind of odd that a woman is trying to pick up guys in this bar? And she's a little to eager if you ask me, probably into some weirdness. That's messed up." Wilbur warns David.

"Come on." Lenny leans over toward David. "Don't you guys read Playboy? Women are into this sex stuff, you know, they're empowered."

"And don't you have to be home tonight to take your kid trick or treating." Wilbur tells David.

"You're right. I'll have a quick beer with her then I'm out the door." David says.

"See that you do." Wilbur tells him as he mixes a martini.

Chapter 2

At David's house, a single leaf wanders across a lawn. Fallen from a tall oak tree in the middle of the front yard, there are still many green leaves clinging to the branches, leaves still infused with chlorophyll. This single leaf has been torn from the vibrant society of the leaves, tumbled to the ground and blown around. The leaf is turning dim green. Sensing the changing season, the tree has released a chemical that severs the leaf from the branch. Disconnected from the tall branches, the leaf wanders the yard, close to the tree but not physically part of the oak any longer. The leaf blows around and around the tree as if waiting for the others in the tree to follow, beckoning them, imploring them to join the other fallen leaves in their ceaseless wandering in the last phase of their existence, soon to decompose and return to the soil.

There was crispness in the air that only the advent of autumn can bring as a light breeze rustles the branches in the tall oak. The tree is as much a part of the landscape as the house it shades, the tree planted and the house built at the same time. The house is an old colonial, two stories with basement. This house used to be part of a small farm; there are even remnants of rock walls and barbed wire fencing around the property. The neighborhood had slowly built up around this house as the area was developed with houses, roads, sidewalks and street lamps. The chimney is slightly separated from the house and puffs out wisps of white smoke that curl over the shingled roof and flow up into the air in the amber dusk. It is cool but not quite as cold as usual for this time of year, the fireplaces are fired up more for effect or habit than comfort. Not that everyone is snuggled away for the evening; there are actually a great many people out in the neighborhood. Both adults and children are emerging from their homes as the sun sets and the evening begins. Dinner is postponed or hastily served and wolfed down. Cars travel down the street of the neighborhood slowly and carefully as some cars pull into driveways and children rush out of the front doors of the houses and scream excitedly. Tugging at sleeves and grabbing briefcases, the children usher their fathers into their houses as mothers follow the children, telling them to calm down and be patient. But the excitement of the children is intoxicating to the fathers as the bad days at offices or factories are pushed to the back of their minds as the gradually energizing fathers tell their children to be patient. But the excitement is so contagious that the fathers smile with boyish grins and tell their children to get their costumes on.

Children, accompanied by mostly fathers, are dressed in all manner of costumes. The kids are dressed as vampires with fake plastic teeth, witches in cardboard hats and old brooms, and cowboys with hats and shiny silver colored plastic six shooters. Some kids have cardboard masks of comic book heroes. A few children have elaborate rubber masks of werewolves. Paper bags in hand, the children singly or in small groups, at first tentatively walk up sidewalks and ring doorbells, or knock softly and hesitantly and utter "trick or treat" but as they go to more houses, they become more confident. The children sneakily eat a little candy bar or other sweet sugary treat as they go from house to house. They become bolder, striding to the door and busting out a "trick or treat" as they punch the bell or rap the door. The youngest and smallest being the cutest of course, have to be coaxed to the door. The parents remind their children to say "thank you" after getting a treat dropped in their bags.

Treats are far more abundant that tricks, except for the intermittent papering of a tree with toilet paper or egging of a house by some immature bad hats that should know better. That is the extent of the tricks played in this neighborhood. Usually, the kids who play pranks are discovered because they brag about it to their friends or other kids at school. But even though throwing toilet paper in someone's tree appears at least superficially to be quite innocuous it is messy and inconsiderate to the homeowner, maybe it relieves some pent up adolescent pressure or maybe it is just bad manners. But they should be made to clean up the mess nonetheless. Or maybe its part of pre-adulthood, creating a tougher persona to set the offender apart from their teenage peers, assuming they are a teenager. Anyone older has other problems if they are pulling such childish pranks. It boils down to getting attention and crudely expressing themselves. Hey! Here I am! I'm in control because I can throw toilet paper or eggs at you house and you have to clean it up! But really the whole prank thing on Halloween is just rude.

Halloween, the pagan holiday, has been co-opted by this country. The roots and history of Halloween conveniently rewritten both for religious and commercial purposes. As long as we package holidays in some quasi-religious wrapper to fit our dogma then we feel more comfortable not only observing it but commercializing the holiday. We have managed to create a holiday where we confront our fears and make a tidy profit as well. Candy sales over Halloween rival Thanksgiving, Christmas, and even Valentines Day for candy volume. Include the costumes sales, parties, cards, and Halloween related movies and television specials and it is a monster of a holiday. Some people might say it is a conspiracy between candy manufacturers, costume companies and media executives to create a marketing frenzy for their products in order to make more money. Some might call that a conspiracy or some people might define it as good business. This is America. It's just good timing and dumb luck. We can take an obscure and ancient celebration rooted in our ancient fear of the unknown or more accurately fear of what the seasons might or might not bring, either feast or famine; and create an incredibly successful commercial holiday. We can consume pounds of sugar in the form of little tasty treats while watching hours of television, plopped down on the sofa in front of a radiation spewing television set. But that is part of the American experience; doing something because some one on TV or in a magazine is doing it. It is a shared experience, granted a weird one but Halloween can be shared with everyone. And if it makes a profit, so much the better. So the next time some kid comes to your door in a President

Richard M. Nixon mask, assuming it's 31 October, open your door and your candy bowl because you both are participating in shared cultural experience that is uniquely American. Which is buying lots of fattening candy, cheaply made costumes, watching lots of television and then running around your neighborhood like a crazed lunatic.

Many parents would be relieved if Halloween night was the scariest thing their children experienced. But parents know the world has many problems and some truly frightening things in it. So they worry about their children. Whether it's how many times their children have had diaper rash or have a fever or how many they have to go to the doctor? Is their school safe? Will their children avoid drugs? When they start driving will their children be safe on the roads? Will their kids get into a nice university like Cornell even though their parents will mortgage the house and never retire?

The popular perception is that mother's worry more than father's. But an argument can be made that fathers worry as much if not more. This may not be readily apparent until you have the situation of a daughter and boyfriend. The CIA should be as thorough. You have to answer fewer questions to get a security clearance than to date some father's daughters. Then there is the threatening posture most fathers try to project, in some cases if the father is a hunter, he will make a point to show the boyfriend the twelve point buck he brought down with one shot from a hundred yards. Or maybe the father played football and tells stories of how many guys he put in the hospital. Or maybe the father is a policeman and tells stories of how he can arrest and throw anyone in jail anytime he wants to. Or maybe the father will make it a point to show off his chain saw and make it known he is not afraid to use it in very creative ways.

Children are running all around the neighborhood, squealing and shrieking. A few have even tried to throw toilet paper up into the tall oak tree in Doris and David Jensen's front yard. So far the young vandals have been thwarted because Delta, the Jensen's daughter has been running to the front window every five minutes to see if her father has arrived home.

"Delta, come back here, sit down and eat your dinner."

"I thought I heard daddy . . ."

"He will be home soon, now sit down and eat your dinner, you're going to be running around all night, now eat.

The young girl reluctantly shuts the curtain and drags her feet across the worn carpet and sits down at the table. When she sits down she gets a static shock due to the dry, fall air.

"Ow!" She immediately bolts up and out of the chair, knocking her knee on the underside of the table, jostling everything on the table.

"Where are you going girl? Sit down." Her exasperated mother tells her.

"I want to do that again!" She shuffles her feet on the carpet, gets a little jolt as she sits back in the chair. "I am eletcro woman!" She states in her deepest voice.

Picking at bits of tuna pasta salad, holding her fork between the thumb and forefinger, she clicks her fork intermittently on the hard Melmac plate. Melmac sounds like some sort of alien planet but is actually a kind of hard plastic made from Melamine which is chemically derived from a pesticide and mixed with formaldehyde to make the plastic. Blissfully unaware of the chemical composition of her plate, Delta takes an absent-minded sip of milk from her nearly full glass, also made of Melmac. On the other side of the round wooden table, an empty plate waits between her and her mother. The door bell rings and the mother walks toward the front door, stops and picks up a huge candy dish on the sideboard by the dining room table, and she glides over to the front door, her knee length cotton and rayon floral print dress twirling in time to her flowing steps. As she opens the door, Doris gets a little static shock that she ignores as a vampire, ghost, and hippy confront her.

"Trick or treat!" They yell in unison, in six-year-old voices.

"Oh!" She gasps in mock horror. "What frightening costumes, here you go. I hope you all like chocolate." The children thank her and run back along the sidewalk to show their parents their candy.

"Delta why don't you get into your costume." Her mother says as she closes the door quietly with a sigh of resignation.

"Is daddy home?" Running halfway to the door.

"No honey, but you need to be ready when he does." She says with a hint of annoyance, not at Delta but at her absent husband.

"Okay, Momma." On a basic level, Delta is attuned to her mother; she senses her mother's annoyance. Most children are in a personal centric frame of mind and believe that the world revolves around them which is a very sensible mindset for children to have.

Delta runs upstairs to put on her costume, while downstairs in the living room, Doris begins to pace back and forth, a nervous habit left over from her battle with quitting cigarettes. She quit smoking when she learned she was pregnant. The nicotine soothed her natural hyperactive personality. But cigarettes were a messy and expensive habit that fit neither her fastidious nature nor her thrifty tendencies. Doris was neat and liked order or at least a semblance of it, not in the extreme to where she wouldn't let Delta be a bit of a tomboy to play and rough house and return home dirty and ragged. But she did keep a clean house and insisted that both Delta and David contribute to that by tidying up and doing their assigned chores. Doris paced back and forth, David was not a punctual person but he would never forget Halloween, he enjoyed it as much as Delta. Maybe he stopped off for a beer with some of his so called co-workers although as far as she could tell, they did as little work as possible. She considered calling his office but he wouldn't be there but she tried anyway. She put the receiver to her ear as her jaw clenched, it rang a few times and someone at the other end answered, "Graphics Department."

"Yes, this is Doris Jansen, I was wondering if David was still there?"

On the other end of the phone there was a pause for a few moments. Finally she heard, "No ma'am, he left quite awhile ago."

"I see, do you know where he went?" As she said that, Doris immediately crunched her eyes shut and rubbed the back of her neck. She did not want to be the shrewish wife.

"Well, I think he and some of the guys were talking about Halloween, their kids costumes, then somebody mentioned they were going to stop at a bar before hitting the candy trail."

"Thank you." She hung up the receiver, perplexed. It was more or less David's habit to stop for a beer but when it came to something involving Delta, even his friends and fermented barley and hops, didn't interfere. Unfortunately, the same couldn't be said for practically everything else in David's and their life. On the other hand maybe he was sitting in some bar throwing back a few brews with his buddies. Women flirting with David. The more she thought about it, the angrier she became.

Delta came floating down the stairs in her Cinderella costume and asked, "Was that daddy, is he going to be late?"

"Yes, yes he is . . ." She trailed off, lying to Delta. How could she tell her that her father probably forgot about one of the most fun and most anticipated events in a child's life? It would be like telling someone they won a million dollars then telling them they get a dollar a year for the next million years. That does not meet expectations. And that can be one of the cruelest things to do, dash someone's expectations. He probably forgot it, just slipped his mind, particularly if he was with some of his buddies. David had to be the center of attention, with his jokes and silly conversation. His personality was full of energy but so misdirected some of the time but it is what attracted her to him as it did other people.

The doorbell rang. Doris grabbed the candy dish, and opened the door to a chorus of trick or treats. She distributed the candy.

"Delta why don't you answer the door until your daddy gets home, please?" Doris was not in a mood to deal with trick or treaters or Halloween this evening. The more she thought about David, the tighter her jaw clenched, teeth involuntarily grinding together till her jaw ached. Still she held her temper in check.

The evening progressed, Delta happily answered the door with hopes of going out herself. Doris sat in her chair pretending to read a magazine while her blood pressure rose such that her forehead seemed to glow like coals in a fireplace. But Delta glided about the room answering the door, handing out candy in her shiny white dress and black shoes with a faux gold tiara perched upon her short red blond hair, freckles sprinkling her nose. This went on for almost an hour. Delta kept so busy, she had not noticed that it was becoming too late for her to go out herself. No children had come to the door for about twenty minutes when it rang again and Delta answered it. Doris just continued to sit in her chair when Delta came over and tapped her shoulder.

"Momma, there is a policeman at the door."

"That's nice honey."

But he wants to see you."

"Just give him some candy that's left, and let's call it a night." She figured it was just a teenager out for some last minute treats but then the small hairs at the back of her neck become to tingle. She stood up, her arms pushing at the handles to the chair, shoulders hunched, her jaw dropped a little parting her lips as she drew in a quick breath then her pupils dilated as her eyes widened. She hurried to the door.

"Mrs. Jansen?" A deep voice came from the direction of the front doorway.

Doris told her daughter to stay in the living room as she went to talk to the officer. Delta saw her mother and policeman talk in the doorway. She couldn't hear their conversation but she saw her mother's reaction, her mother's face turned white, the blood drained as the policeman talked. The policeman placed his hand on her arm as if to steady her. As she turned away from the policeman, Delta saw a strange mix of emotion on her mother's face. An expression that Delta had seen only a few times like when Delta had went to her friend's house, crossing the street without asking permission. The same expression her mother had that day was the same as today except mixed with held back tears. With a deep breath, Doris turned back to the policeman; she nodded as they talked in quiet voices. The rest of the night and a few days after that were just a blur. The kind of blur where they couldn't remember what they did on any particular day. Their lives changed. It was to be the third most memorable Halloween for Delta as it turned out.

Chapter 3

Under a full moon, the wind pushed the tree branches until they creaked. The trees were losing leaves in great bunches; the brown, desiccated leaves blew and eventually floated to the brown lawn below. Waves of leaves were forming up and were blown across the sidewalk and collided with the house sometimes with enough force that they splashed up against the exterior wall, exploding up in a an orange and brown spray that reached up to the windows. The swaying trees and whipping leaves cast shadows that swept into Doris's bedroom. Doris lay on her back in bed, staring up at the ceiling, mesmerized by the play of moonlight and the shadows on the white ceiling. Doris stared at the ceiling. After awhile, she turned her head to one side, to the night stand, the clock showed 5:00 AM. Out of habit she nearly turned to the other side of the bed but she stopped herself because she knew there would be nobody there. That was not a new occurrence, David had worked many night shifts. Or so he told her. There had always been a kernel of doubt about those late nights, strange shift hours. Particularly when she had awakened and he was not there beside her. All sorts of scenarios presented themselves such as another woman or he was out drinking or maybe he was in an accident. That last thought sickened her because it almost made her laugh. That was irony wasn't it? Many nights she had thought he was in a bar someplace, or the victim of some workplace accident. Maybe one of the shipping crates had fallen on him when he went out to the factory floor or in a drunken driving accident like she had read about so often in the papers. Is that the definition of prescient, she could foresee terrible accidents or was it because if you assume the worse, you are correct sooner or later. Best not to dwell on any of those things early in the morning when all the horrible possibilities seem terrifyingly possible. Sleep had been elusive but Doris could put those negative thoughts aside and think of more practical manners because that was her strength and everyone, including her family or anyone that knew her, knew she had that ability to shut everything and everyone out to focus on just what was in front of here.

A checklist began to formulate in her mind which she would write down shortly but she allowed herself the luxury of lying in bed. She had of course called her mother to come sit with Delta while she went to the hospital last night. Fortunately, her mother was home and came right over. The police met her at the hospital since she had turned down the offer of a ride. Even as she walked to her car, there were still a few witches and goblins running around, a few houses were egged and pumpkins with candles still burning with leering faces. All along her drive to the hospital, there was Halloween all around her.

She knew how to get to the hospital; it was the same one that Delta was born in. She parked her car near the Emergency Room entrance and pulled her coat around her. The double doors opened for her as she stepped on the black rubber pad. The policeman was waiting. He was three years younger than Doris and the picture of what tax payers want their Highway Patrolman to look like. He was over six feet, closely cropped hair that seem molded for his hat, and looked like the kind of guy you would want giving you a hand up if you were clinging to a cliff. He was still talking with the ER doctor, a middle age man whose bags under his eyes made him look much older.

"Hey doc, this is probably the lady coming in. The DOA we brought in."

The doctor glanced up from scribbling on a clipboard of papers, as the patrolman continued. "Should I stay here or go back with you guys? I need to talk over the situation with her."

"First DOA case?" The doctor inquired.

"Yea, I mean, I've seen accidents before, but they pulled through. This guy and the woman with him were just torn up. It was hard to tell there were people in the car."

All right then. If you throw up, do it in a waste basket. I'm not in the mood to clean up after you." The doctor exhales a long breath. "Seems like we're seeing more and more of these auto cases. I don't remember it like this in med school."

"Why's that?"

I don't know. Fast cars, martinis and asphalt are a real bad combination." The doctor says wearily.

Doris has slowly walked up to the reception desk where the policeman and doctor were standing, taking her coat off and draping it over the same arm as her handbag. The doctor takes a step forward, toward Doris. "Ma'am, thanks for coming down, I know this is a difficult time for you." The doctor does his best to sound concerned and not jaded.

The patrolman interjects, "As I mentioned to you, we do have his wallet but I'm afraid we need a positive ID from you. Has anyone else besides you and your husband been driving the car?"

"No."

"Does . . . did he usually stop off after work anywhere?"

"Sometimes."

"I'm sorry but I need to ask you some more questions." He grabs a large manila envelope and opens it and pulls out a shredded, stained blue shirt with David's name embroidered on it. "Does this look like your husband's shirt from work?"

She recognizes it immediately, it was part of the uniform he was required to wear. There were only a handful of people at the plant that wore a blue shirt. "Yes."

"Secondly, this is your husbands work identification and wallet?"

Just a glance is all it takes. She nods and asks, "What about his wedding ring and watch?"

Officer Rueben digs back into the manila folder and doesn't find them. Kind of odd. He makes a mental note to check with the detective. He figures David probably slipped it in his pocket if he was out picking up women since he still had his fingers, they were horribly mangled but attached. The watch is probably back at the station or still out on the highway. "I'm sorry ma'am, there not here but I'll check on it. I'm sorry to question you like this, it's just that we have to follow up. Such as verifying identity. There will be more I'm afraid, sorry."

"Can I look at him?"

"That's not a good idea . . . maybe after the funeral home would be better." The doctor interrupts but he really didn't think that anyone could do much to make the face or the body remotely recognizable. David shot thru the windshield and onto the pavement, essentially skinning himself alive. The firemen had to sweep up his skin. And what was left of his body was like picking up a sack of busted up steak bones. "He had significant head trauma." Is all the doctor says.

"But still I could . . ."

"I know this is a difficult for you." The doctor does his best to sound concerned rather than just tired.

The patrolman interrupts, "But has there been anyone else that drives his car?"

"No, well I do and some of his buddy's have driven his car. Why do you want to know?" Some of his slacker friends from high school she thinks bitterly to herself. Beer swilling, Neanderthals that never grew out of their teen years, they had no roots, didn't care about anything but their next six-pack.

"So, someone else could have been driving his car?"

"No, he was coming home tonight, it was Halloween . . ."

"Does you husband usually stop off after work at a tavern or anything."

"Sometimes"

"OK ma'am, I'm sorry to ask you a question you like this, it's just that we need to verify these things. And I apologize for asking this. Did your husband maybe have someone he meets at the bar?"

"Sure, quite a few of his co-workers, he knew the bartender, I think . . . but that's not what you're asking, is it?"

"I was thinking more of maybe female friends."

"What? You mean a girlfriend? No, I would have known. I think."

"Sorry about that but just have to go through these questions."

"I want to see my husband."

"That's not a good idea. Your husband suffered massive head trauma." The doctor injects again.

"But I still could . . ." she trails off.

The doctor picks up the conversation. "I can't stop you but there is very little you would recognize. We may have to resort to dental records."

"David didn't have a dentist."

"I just think it would be too traumatic for you Mrs. Jansen. I would call and make arrangements with a home perhaps they can do something." Although he doubted it. The man was severely mangled in the crash; it would be like assembling a jig saw puzzle.

"A funeral home, I really hadn't thought."

"It's fine, the receptionist has a list." The doctor points back across the room to a huge credenza with a white haired, older lady behind it.

Doris turns and walks over to her. The patrolman says to the doctor in a hushed voice as Doris moves away. "So you're not taking her back?"

"No, unless you need visual ID, I would rather not."

"Well, everything matches, the clothes, height and weight match his drivers license, and it's his car. I may have to ask her about the girl in the car with him but I'll do that later if I need to. I still have to find out who the Jane Doe is. I don't think the wife will be much help to ID her."

"Nope, the wife is always the last to know." The doctor says without humor. "I guess that wraps this up for us, not her."

"I know, I guess."

"What do you mean, you guess? The doctor says flipping through the pages on his clipboard.

"The time doesn't add up . . . they left the bar and then what? If they're that horny they would stopped at the first motel. Doesn't quite figure. Off by at least twenty minutes. And now the wedding ring and the watch."

"Wedding ring?"

"She's right. A guy always has his wedding ring. One thing a guy is not going to do is lose his wedding ring. It should have been on his finger or in his pocket. And that lost time. That bugs me."

"So what could happen in those few minutes? Maybe they couldn't wait and pulled over. Maybe the other motels didn't have a vacancy? So they were driving too fast to get to some motel and then crash. The ring flies off his hand. It's on the highway someplace. Come on Rueben, you see a conspiracy in every case since you took that detective exam." The doctor grins at him.

"Yeah I guess but there were a bunch of cheap motels, why not stop at one of those? But guess you're right. Maybe I'm over thinking this. What about the woman in the other car?" The policeman inquires.

"Don't remind me. That was a mess. The husband is on his way. How do you tell a guy he's lost his wife? All because people get hammered and get behind the wheel. There should be a law." The doctor says wearily. "But just like the other two, not much left to identify."

"Oh yeah, that's right." He trails off.

"This night gets better and better." The doctor tells the policeman and himself. "My advice, don't string this out any longer than you have to and make it more complicated than it is. Just going to cause more agony for these folks."

"It's probably nothing, so he stopped off at a bar and had a girl on the side, I don't want to tell his wife but I'm going to have to. I still have to identify the blonde Jane Doe with him. She had no identification. In my experience somebody that doesn't have at least a driver's license or some identification is up to something. My gut tells me these two were up to something. Maybe I should take her back to look at the girl . . ."

"Of course they were up to something but you don't need to spell it out in slimy detail for the wife. My medical evaluation doesn't dispute anything in your report. But I don't see any reason to show her the mess on the slabs back there."

"Yeah, I guess we've taken this as far as we can on this one. But don't you think it's strange she just heard about her husband and isn't crying?"

"Not really, she's in shock and different people react differently to stress."

"Spooky."

"There are several stages to the grief process and everyone deals with it a bit differently and in their own time, so no it's not unusual."

"But this woman is just spooky. Didn't cry or anything when I told her."

"I've seen all the categories of grief stricken women come through here. You have your mothers which are particularly gut wrenching if it's a child involved." The doctor rubs his temples. "You're right most women cry inconsolably. But not all. All that BS about women being the weaker sex, don't you believe it."

"Come on doc." He says with a grin.

"Oh, I'll concede that women may be more emotional but you do a rotation through the maternity ward, and then talk to me about tough."

"Well I hope she is tough because she has got troubles, doc."

"She's coming back over." The policeman says in a very quiet tone then in a voice that Doris can hear, as he stands next to the doctor.

"I don't think we need a visual ID on him." He turns to Doris as she walks up. "I'm sorry ma'am; did you get some arrangements made?"

"Yes, I suppose so, I guess . . ."

"It will be a couple of days before we can release your husband but if you need help just call me, here's my card," He hands her his business card with Officer R. Rueben printed on it. "We can get our report completed as quick as we can."

"Do you need anything else for your report?" The doctor asks.

"I'll check with my sergeant but we may have a few more questions." The officer states as he glances over at the doctor. The doctor rolls his eyes and shakes his head just a little.

"I need to go home now, if that's not a problem. My little girl is at home, my mother is staying with her but I need to get home." Doris replies.

"Of course, ma'am." The officer says. As she walks away, he gets this little nagging ache in the back of his head. It's a simple case. Guy cheats on wife with a bar room blonde, gets in a wreck rushing to some motel, end of story. So what bothers him about this case?

Chapter 4

Every place does have a distinctive scent. Hospitals and morgues and funeral homes have an antiseptic smell but it's a complex scent. Hints of a metallic, copper smell underneath the ammonia smell; a faint stench of death no matter how clean they are, attaches to these places. Of course hospitals invoke fear and sadness but fear and sadness tempered by hope because hospitals are where we go to get our bodies repaired, at least most of the time. Morgues and funeral homes just invoke fear and sadness. Our sense of smell is one of our most unappreciated senses except when we come across a skunk or forget to take out the garbage with the rotten eggs, but it is the one sense that can sneak up on us and flood our minds with feelings that we never knew were there, lurking just below our conscious perception. With sight, well you see things coming, a fastball high and tight, you have at least a split second to react. Or with touch, if you grab the biscuits out of the oven without a potholder, your hand will recoil in an autonomic reaction before the brain can react. If you go to a rock concert, your hands instinctively go to your ears to protect them as much as possible for the high decibel noise. With taste, there is little that can surprise our taste buds, each one assigned to tell if something is sweet, sour, and leaves it up to our mind to determine whether the taste is palatable or not. With all of these senses there is some warning before the experience, we know if we are going to eat and drink, our sight is our sensor that scans our environment to do just that, warn us, and our hearing is another sense connected to our brain to guide us through a world full of stairs, traffic, cliffs, hot stoves and coffee, hurricane sirens, rap music, countless number of hazards. All of these senses are like the radar on a ship guiding it over the sea. But the sense of smell seems to bypass some of the pragmatic responses that guide us through life rather than keeping us from stumbling into a curb or into traffic, the sense of smell is connected directly to our emotions. Sense of smell does assist us, but has evolved into something more than a mere indicator of our immediate environment. It is an emotional barometer. Walking down the sidewalk to the store, you can catch a whiff of perfume from somewhere, and the memory of the first person you loved floods back. It may have been the thing furthest from your mind, but it comes back in such vivid detail. Smell invokes the feelings of the experience as if it was five minutes ago; sometimes you can even feel the touch, the taste, see the sights and hear the sounds. That is the power of the sense of smell.

Doris and another woman wait in the foyer of a building hesitating to proceed any further. The building is built in the style of a Georgia plantation manor house complete with faux marble columns. There is a chandelier hanging down from the high ceiling that drops down between a split staircase like an impossibly huge diamond in the cleavage of a dowager dressed in her gaudiest evening gown. The other, older woman is David's mother, she fidgets with a large, shoulder purse, snapping and unsnapping the large clasp that opens into the cavernous maw of the bag. Inside are cigarettes, four lighters—three are empty, mounds of make up, tissues, and an assortment of folded and wadded up papers—chewing gum wrappers, used tissues, pieces of paper with names, numbers, addresses on them, receipts, and dry cleaning receipts. The bag droops from her shoulder, one hand busy with the clasp and the other hand lightly touches her poofy dyed black hair to ensure not a strand has strayed. The powder blue dress she wears with pearls does complement her hair and slightly doughy figure. Her eyes, red, can't be concealed by the make up.

"Melba, please stop playing with your purse." Doris says and the woman stops.

"This is a very nice place, they will do a good job for my boy, I know they will, won't they?" She begins sniffling; she digs into her purse in a vain search for a clean tissue.

"Of course, ma'am. We will do our utmost," A silky voice says from one of the side hallways. A little startled, they had not heard the man join them in the foyer. Dressed in a dark suit and muted blue tie, the man spoke in hushed tones, used in mortuaries. Also, it is difficult to judge a morticians age, perhaps it is the chemicals they use or perhaps the juxtaposition between the living and the dead. But some morticians seem as artificial as some of the flowers.

"I'm sorry, I hope I didn't disturb you, Mycroft Myles." He extends his hands and grasps Doris's hand in a soft two handed clasp. "You spoke on the phone to one of my associates, Mrs. Jansen."

Doris takes his hand while he grasps firmly, "If you could just step this way, we can go to my office." But before he leads them down one of the side hallways, he looks sympathetically at Melba. "You must be the mother, I'm so sorry for your loss."

Melba sniffles a reply.

From the sunlight in the foyer, Mr. Myles leads them down a progressively dimmer, dark wood paneled hallway to his office. An organ plays quietly in the background somewhere in the building, probably a recording, playing a familiar song, but one you can't quite place. He ushers them into his office, closing the door. Pulling out cushy chairs for both of the women, he sits down in front of his desk, he glides down into the seat of his leather high back chair.

"I know in this, your time of great sorrow," He pauses as he slides around to the right side of the desk to open a drawer, "words are but of small comfort." He pulls from the desk drawer a portfolio of various options and their prices. He loves these mid western yokels they usually try to go the Egyptian route and build monuments to their loved ones and Mr. Myles is more than ready to assist them as long as their check clears. Like his father, who moved from Chicago to the south to find an under served area, he had found this little niche.

The director of the funeral home settles himself behind the desk as he ponders these two grieving women. Obviously one is the wife and the other the mother. After years in this business, he hardly needs to ask anymore. He prides himself on personally interviewing each one of the clients regardless of their financial profile because everyone can beg, borrow or steal money for a funeral which from a strict business viewpoint has served his interests quite effectively. Although he is quite proficient at the technical and artistic side of his profession, such as the embalming and makeup, it is always the personal touch that makes or breaks a business concern. And this is the part of the business he enjoys the most. Sometimes he thinks it's a bit morbid the way he seems to feed on the sorrow of his client's families but it's a morbid business.

Meeting with families is one of the critical details. But the most critical detail is money. His clients can't take it with them and let's be honest; most people can't stand their relatives so why leave them any money. Mr. Myles considers his unabashed avarice as one more service that he provides for his deceased client. Contrary to popular belief, the gaunt, vulture man in an ill fitting suit is not what the industry is about. That is why he got his business degree to augment his career and it has been very beneficial. It has definitely been a lucrative addition to his professional capabilities.

His years of practical knowledge, he gathered from working in the funeral home for his father. At an early age, what was it ten or twelve years old? He started working in the funeral home, not in back at first but after a few months his father brought him to the embalming room and showed him the core of the business. It's about moving product with a human touch his father used to say. Mr. Myles always kept that phrase in mind when he started his businesses. And particularly when he went back to personally attend to his father in the embalming room. He even convinced his own mother to pay for the platinum burial package even though he inherited his father's mortuary. Both his businesses, the mortuary he started and the one he inherited, are doing extremely well but he has plans. But Mr. Myles is going corporate and opening establishments all around the area, turning his business into a mortuary moneymaker.

Mr. Myles turns his perfect smile to Doris and Melba. The bird in hand.

"I have taken the liberty of putting together a package for you that from my extensive experience serves your needs." He slides a light blue folder across the polished wood desktop to Doris. She glances down at it and reaches forward but it seems like she is pushing her hand through cold gelatin to reach the folder. She pulls it closer end opens it, she feels as if her entire body is moving thru gelatin, each movement seems heavy, she wonders if Melba and this Mycroft notice. Everything moves slower, voices sound muted, motion seems to be at a crawl while her mind seems to be spinning with disparate emotions; sadness, anger, fear, hate, love and all of them felt in different combinations and intensity that makes her dizzy. She knows the funeral director has been talking about something and her mind is racing to process the information but the sound is not getting to ears fast enough for her mind to process. She needs to focus . . .

" . . . and as I said previously, this is one of our most poplar models, and if I may express an observation, many people have picked this particular one to hold their loved ones forever . . ."

"Oh, Doris, what do you think of this one?"

Melba points to a picture of the casket in the blue brochure that Mr. Myles had presented them.

"It's nice I suppose." What a strange thing to say she thinks.

"I do like the color, the glossy gray metal finish, do you have one here we can look at?' Melba asks.

"Of course, I believe we have one in stock and if I recall it may be last year's model." He scratches his chin and continues. "I may even be able to give you a discount, assuming I still have it and it's not on lay away for another client. I can also include a protective coating."

"I really like it. What about the fabric, is it felt?"

"It's a synthetic silk like blend I believe."

"I see." Says Melba as she leafs through the brochure, the suddenly, "Oh my goodness!"

"What is it Mrs. Jansen? Myles inquires soothingly as he reaches across the desk and puts his hand on her hand. Doris looks over at Melba.

"I just realized, what will David wear? I'm not even sure he has a tie."

"Yes, he does." Doris replies but doesn't add to the conversation by saying he wore a tie to their wedding and to church. He really had no need for a suit.

"Well. We may need something special." Melba replies.

"I work with Miller Clothiers in town. They have tuxedos, suits, an exceptional array of fine clothes and we have worked with them extensively."

"Marvelous." Melba claps her hands together like a little girl who is trying to dress her doll with a stack of new clothes.

"I don't think it's necessary."

"Oh Doris, we can go through your closets but are we really going to find anything appropriate?"

"It just happens that I have one of Millers business cards, here you can call on them and tell them you are working with us and they will give you a significant discount." He slides the card to Melba.

"Thank you."

"Now you will see in the brochure an itemized list of the prices, the numbers in red are non-negotiable items that we have to provide per various ordinances both county and state. But the others are options." There were plenty of red numbers.

Doris looks over Melba's shoulder at the thousands of dollars for base prices for the different packages. Their insurance policy can pay for the funeral but not if the funeral costs keep adding up, and she doesn't have a job yet. She hasn't had a job since high school, she was a waitress. How can they survive on that kind of salary? What about their savings? That is a cruel joke, their savings is a few hundred in the bank."

"What's this?" Melba points to an item on the options list. "What's a vault? Do people break into graves?"

"No, no." He says with a hint of a chuckle, the first genuine emotion he has expressed. "No that's to protect the deceased from the harsh underground environment for as long as possible."

"How much would that be?" Melba turns in her chair to address Doris. "Honey, how much was the insurance again?"

Mycroft has to take his handkerchief out because he nearly starts salivating. Clients with insurance money.

"Let me see, the size of coffin, approximate parameters of the site, and let's see, I assume you want a concrete enclosure for the vault?" He says as he writes down figures on the paper.

"Well, yes I suppose so." Says Melba hesitantly.

"That will be an additional $890, but with the discount I'm giving you, that allows you to add the vault."

"Marvelous." Says Melba.

"Now let's discuss the headstone, what sort of marble are you interested in? The ordinary or something of higher quality?"

She begins to emerge out of her daze as the reality of her situation and the fact that she has to make a living to support herself and Delta. To raise a daughter and support a household. They did have the life insurance policy, a benefit of David working at the plant, a substantial bit of money but Doris knows they can't live off that forever. She is now the sole provider for her daughter. David isn't around and she has to do everything now. Its just like David is goofing off somewhere, dreaming about building a park or painting some landscape or building their dream house while she is left to do the dull work of day to day life. She can't afford to spend a fortune burying David. She needs the money to live, because if she doesn't . . . they might not.

"Screw it."

"Excuse me."

"Doris!" Melba says

"No I mean it, screw the whole damn thing." She almost rises from her chair as she sits up and forward in her seat. "I have some of insurance money, I will use some of it, but that is for everything; headstone, burial, service, and that's it." She is grateful that their insurance both the life and car insurance were paid up, it pays for this and some other debts. Maybe she and her daughter will have a little money to carry them over.

"Now, I know you're upset, Mrs. Jansen." He looks over at Melba and gives her a little nod as if to say I've dealt with many grieving spouses this is not a problem.

"I'm not upset." She says calmly.

"There are various stages of grief we go through, and it's healthy to express those feelings, in fact I encourage my clients to let themselves express those feelings."

"Which clients are those? The ones you plant in the ground or the ones you bury in a mound of contract double talk?" One hand gripping the arm of the chair and the other hand forcefully striking the other arm of the chair.

"This is the grief talking. I'm sure normally you're quite a reasonable . . ."

"You really want to know what I'm feeling right now?" I've got news for you mister, my life is never going to be normal again and I'm already tired of taking crap from you not to mention . . . Well anyway, you've done nothing but patronize me since I stepped in the door, maybe that's how it normally works, I don't know and I don't really care. I'm here to arrange to bury my husband. But you've done nothing but dump new problems on me."

"Still, Mrs. Jansen, I'm here to help." He can feel the normal dynamic of this meeting changing. He looks over at Melba but it is like looking into the face of someone after they've fallen overboard as the ship slips further and further away.

"Look here." She takes the forefinger of each of her hands, she points to her eyes." Look into these eyes; do I look like I need your kind of help?"

He looks into the dark brown, dry eyes.

"Now what I need is a funeral and one I can afford and that's not going to cause me and my kid to be living on the street, because we can't pay the mortgage on our house because we have some huge marble monstrosity over my husband."

"Again Mrs. Jansen, there are certain items that I must charge . . ."

"Like what, the vault? Gone he doesn't need that. The concrete? Gone." She had pulled the folder with the cost figures from Melba's hands. "What's this? Clean and vacuum the coffin? You're joking? Gone, a little dirt isn't a problem. As for his clothes, David had a nice tie and trousers he wore to church, plus . . ." She pauses here and tears do begin to appear in the corners of her eyes. "It will be a closed casket." Doris's face goes ashen but in a moment the color is back. "I think I will put him in jeans and a shirt, he will be comfortable."

"Doris, dear, show some respect, he was my son and your husband."

"Respect? What your son did . . . I . . . Melba what he did, how can we ever . . . ." Melba recoils as Doris cringes at the thought of how her husband died and what they must live with, all of them including Delta. "I'm sorry that was out of line. You don't deserve that, none of us, not you, me, or Delta."

"I appreciate your feelings and financial position but perhaps there is an installment plan we can work out. At a modest interest rate." Doris looks over at him and her teeth begin to clench like a pair of pliers.

"Okay." She says and Mr. Myles smiles thinly. "Where's my husband? We're leaving. You can put him in the station wagon and we will take him someplace else. I would like to conduct a bit of comparison shopping." Melba gasps but says nothing.

"What?" He stammers, eyes open wide blinking. In all his years, no one has ever said that. "Madam, you just can't leave."

"Why not?"

Well . . ." He thinks for a Moment. "It's not legal, we have incurred costs . . ."

"Fine, I'll pay your blackmail but, one thing you can be sure of . . . I will check all these so called county and state laws that you say have to charge me for."

"If you will just calm down, we can discuss this rationally. I realize you have been under a great deal of stress."

"Calm down, you want me to calm down after you are essentially holding my dead husband for ransom. Okay, what's the ransom for his release, what's the price for my husband? Can you tell me that? Do you size up people from all your experience in the business? Maybe you have a friend down at the bank that can tell you that the family is rich so you can charge them an arm and a leg but I'm poor so how much do you think you can get away with charging me? Rich people can have rich funerals Mr. Myles but I'm not rich, I will be literally living hand to mouth. And no, I am not going to borrow the money, not from family, not friends, and certainly not from the bank. Mr. Myles this is difficult for me, not just my husband's death, but the fact that I simply can't give him a better funeral than what I've said. You tell me what the price is, it can't be the same for everyone. Maybe all people are created equal but from what I've seen, they certainly don't end up equal. My husband had a good heart in him from the very first day I met him. He was juvenile and a little irresponsible. But he had integrity and when it came to the important stuff, you could usually depend on him. Or at least I liked to think so. He wanted to see the best in everyone he came across. There was this pan handler in town that claimed to have a broken back and couldn't move his legs but most folks new the guy was a fake, every evening this pan handler would get up and walk off, to home I guess. David would give the guy his spare change even after I told him at breakfast one morning that he was being a stupid patsy and they should run the pan handler off. Rather than get angry at me or the beggar, he just looked up from the sports page and said to me; the guys gotta be hard up to beg for a few coins, I figure if he wants to sit outside for eight or ten hours, that's a hard life and I don't need to make it any harder." She stops and puts a hand to her mouth and calmly sits there, silently for a moment then speaks.

"Mr. Myles, the bottom line is I only have a bit of cash for everything and I will not use up his life insurance and I will not go into debt for this . . . can we work out a deal or do I need to leave?"

He cleared his throat. He would never be certain if he dealt with her because she out maneuvered him or he simply wanted to get rid of this irritating woman.

It's times like these and customers like this that makes him wish he had stayed with his father's funeral home down in the south. At least the rubes were polite. He also wished he hadn't changed his name to Mycroft. But it sounded intelligent and unusual; the Midwestern yokels lapped it up and said how they had never heard that name before. Apparently they never read a Sherlock Holmes story but they still assumed it was British and after awhile he found himself adopting a slight accent. It wasn't a very good accent but he sprinkled his conversations with phrases like "yank' or 'across the pond'. And like the British, he knows when the war is lost.

"Very well then, yes, I think we can deal on those terms." He sighs in surrender.

Chapter 5

The rain pelted the windowsill of Delta's bedroom. She laid on her stomach, across her bed, elbows resting on a pillow, her chin resting on cupped hands as she looked out the window. The rain seemed to fall from forever or at least that's the way it appeared to Delta. Particularly at night when you couldn't see the clouds, so it appeared the rain fell from a blackness of infinite depth and therefore maybe had an infinite supply of rain drops. Rain can have a very soothing effect, a reassuring effect. But some of the time rain is accompanied by thunder and lightning. When there's a storm it is not the rain that sent Delta running for the security of her parent's bed. But this storm had neither. Just a slow mournful splattering of water against the windows. Even though this rain storm had no thunder and lightning, she kept waiting for it, waiting to be scared. There had been several weeks with periodic rain; the rain at night helped her sleep but not tonight. She stared out the window at the rain, sometimes there were just a few drops, and other times a constant patter of rain and occasionally sheets of water fell. But after observing the rain, she noticed the drops never hit the same spot, nor splatter quite the same. Each drop was unique or appeared to be. Sometimes the drops would hit in succession like marbles falling from a hand, tapping the window tentatively. Other times the wind blown rain would pound the window as if frustrated that that it could not enter Delta's room. And other times just the lonely patter of a rain drop, tired and spent.

Her bedroom window was in the back of the house, so Delta didn't see the headlights of her Grandmother Melba's station wagon. She did hear her mother and grandmother enter through the front door of the house. Her maternal grandmother and grandfather, Joe and Anna, had stood inside the front door waiting for Doris and Melba. For the last hour or so, Joe and Anna had routinely parted the curtains of the window overlooking the driveway to peer out and see if the car they heard outside was the one they so anxiously waited for. Delta heard the familiar steps of her mother on the stairs and then in the hallway. Delta quickly spun around in her bed with her pillow, slipped under the covers and lay down so she looked like she was sleeping. Doris opened Delta's bedroom door just a crack, a harsh sliver of light from the hallway penetrated her room. Doris just wanted some reassurance that Delta was okay. Delta heard a relieved sigh with a hint of melancholy as her mother shut the door. With a certain boldness that surprised her, Delta kicked the cover off that she had so hastily thrown on when her mother arrived back home. When her parents said time for bed, it was time for bed, no procrastination, no negotiation. But she felt some things had changed.

At first she heard the noise as the television blared downstairs but someone turned it off or the volume lower. She slipped out of bed dressed in her pink PJs. She slowly opened her door and heard a loud knocking, more of a pounding on their front door down stairs. She crept out of her bedroom to the top of the stairs. It was the first time she had done this. Her grandfather opened the front door and two people, a man and a woman, stepped into the hall. Her mother glanced down at the floor and not really at the two people. Delta couldn't hear what they were discussing as the group downstairs stepped into the living room. But she could hear muffled voices. While she couldn't hear the words, she could tell who was talking and the emotions in the voices. The woman was sobbing while she talked and the man's voice was strained. Her mother's voice was muted as she shook her head and had certain contriteness in it that Delta had never heard. Her mother had always had a certain conciseness and no nonsense tone to her voice. Delta's maternal grandparents and paternal grandmother were silent. After a few minutes, the adults came out from the living room walked to the front door, the woman was in tears and the man had a blank look on his face as he nodded to Doris as she opened the door for them. As the two people stepped out, the policeman that had accompanied Doris to the hospital arrived on their porch and asked to come in.

Officer Rueben speaks first, "I'm sorry folks, you really shouldn't be here . . ."

"No its okay." Doris interrupts him. "It's okay." The two people nod and leave. Doris lets the officer in the house. She closes the door.

Delta just stood at the top of the stairs and her mother, looking up, somehow regained her normal composure. Delta ducked back around the top of the stairs and into the shadows. All she could hear was muffled voices and a door closing. After a few minutes, her mother calls to her. Delta comes down the stairs, only Doris and the policeman are standing there.

"Delta, its okay honey, come on down."

Delta didn't get completely down the stairs, when her mother rushed over and up the first few steps and hugged Delta as she descended the stairs.

"Momma, I'm sorry I'm up so late, . . . "

"It's okay, It's okay." Her mother said as she hugged Delta, and scooped her up and carried her down the remaining stairs. "You can sit with us for a while." Her mother tells her with a hint of tears in the corner of her eyes, again something that Delta had not often seen.

The officer turned to leave, but turns back around, "I'm sorry about that visit, I told them not to come over but you know it's a small town so knowing where you live wasn't difficult. I want you to know the Police report will determine who is at fault. Just to give you a heads up." Doris nods in appreciation as he continues. "And the report will be made available to families of everyone concerned." He tells her and then adds. "Ma'am did your husband have a life insurance policy?"

"What?"

"Life insurance." He asks again.

"Yes. He did."

"Okay."

"You need it for the report? I can get the policy." She asks.

"No, not really, I was just curious. I'll let myself out." He turns toward the door but hesitates and turns around again. "Excuse me, but did you ever find your husband's ring?"

She looks at him for a moment and replies, "I was thinking of asking you that same question."

Chapter 6

Delta, Doris, Joe, Anna, and Melba, went into the living room. Joe and Melba sat in chairs at the coffee table across from the sofa. Doris and Anna took opposite ends of the sofa while Delta took the middle snuggling against her mother with her legs curled up on the cushions and her feet lightly resting against Anna. Delta's head rests on Doris shoulder, while she caresses the youngster's somewhat tangled, shoulder length hair. They all sit there silently, collectively catching their breath and eventually look around at each other trying to think of something to say. Finally Melba speaks.

"Well that was some stunt your daughter pulled today at the funeral parlor." She says with grudging admiration. Melba tells Doris's parents the story. Towards the end, a big grin erupts on the otherwise melancholy face of Doris as she begins to giggle then laugh. For a few seconds till she haltingly stops and says, "Well, that is one more guy that's sorry he ever met me!"

"Honey, that's not true . . ." Anna begins.

"No I didn't mean it that way, I guess . . ." Although she is not quite sure.

"What I meant was, short story, is I got an incredible deal on the funeral."

"That's my girl." Her father retorts.

"Well, yeah, I'll be able to keep the wolves at bay for a little while and keep bread and I do mean bread, on the table."

"Doris, I've been thinking, we have been thinking, your Mom and me, about what you're going to do."

"What I need to do, is get a job."

"That's what I'm getting at . . ."

"What your father is trying to say is that we want you to work at the hardware store."

"Come on you guys, I do your tax returns, that place is barely breaking even, you get no salary as it is dad. You can't pay any employees."

"I have been thinking of expanding, just not basic hardware but lumber and power tools."

"It takes a lot of money to capitalize something like that." Doris replies.

"I know honey." He says

"But what we could do, is take out a second mortgage and take that money and put back in the business." Her mother states.

"Mom are you sure about that? It's risky." Doris says. "I don't think it's a good move, Mom. But I do have an idea. We have David's life insurance money and this house. We could sell the house and take that money and the insurance money and invest in the store."

"Honey, we can't let you give us that money."

"Your father's right hon, David and you worked yourselves ragged on this house."

"I know but it's the only thing we have, we never were able to save much." She remembers back to David's spending habits, not that he bought for himself but when he got a project in mind like their home, he went full bore into getting the best lumber, the latest fixtures which ironically may be one of the best selling points for their home. That is not what they had in anticipated. The house would have been the place they were to raise Delta but that won't happen.

"Where would you live?" Her father asks.

"Well . . ." Doris begins.

"Of course you would live us, we have plenty of room." Her mother interjects as she looks askance at her husband as he realizes the obvious.

"Well David fixed this place up pretty good, so it should sell, and our house is big enough and is closer to the store." Her father ticks off the list.

"I know." She considers this as she looks over at the stairway that David spent so many hours on, a work of art more than a carpentry job. He must have shaped and sanded at least half a dozen versions of the banister until he got it just the way he had seen it in his mind and his dreams.

As Delta drifts off to a light slumber and the voices in the room become a jumble of mumbles, she dreams of her father. Nestled between Doris and Anna, Delta remembers her dad working on the stairway on another Halloween and then he was going to take her out to trick or treating. That was when she had a fascination with a television show about a cyborg. She imitated the show including the slow motion running and jumping that was part of the special effects of the used to represent the super fast running and jumping ability. She particularly liked the jumping. The astronaut cyborg would leap onto the top of a five story building. Even though she was young; she was bright and not overly naive. Delta had figured out that it was really a man jumping off the building backward and then also running the film backward to make it appear that he was actually jumping up. She still had a little problem with the landing though, she was sure that someone couldn't jump off a building and not get hurt. So she was still trying to figure out the landing part.

On that Halloween, she had watched her father working on the stairway as he pretended he didn't know what day it was. She in turn had humored him and squealed in delight when he had gotten up from his work and stomped up to the top of the stairs where she was sitting. He reached down and grabbed her nose, pretending to pull it off her face, his thumb wiggling as it protruded between his forefinger and index finger.

"Got your nose squirt."

"Oh, daddy!"

"What are you all dressed up for?" He grinned at her. She was in a gray jump suit, supposedly modeled after an astronaut suit. Doris had found the pattern and cloth somewhere and done the sewing.

"It's getting dark daddy!" She says with urgency.

"So it is. I guess its bed time." He replies with a mock yawn.

"No, it's Halloween, it's time to trick or treat."

"Hey, you're right; I guess I'd better get a costume."

"Daddy!"

He had incredible patience and passion, he spent weeks just removing the old paint and varnish from the old stair way railing, to get to the bare wood, the prime timber that he had faith was still there underneath the years of old paint. It was heavy old growth oak. Delta was right beside him most of the time as he sat there, repairing the stairway or some other part of the house.

He took good care of his tools. He kept the scraper sharp, filed to just the right edge, it was a tool he used to take the top layers of old paint, carefully because even though lead abatement was still not widely prevalent, just as a craftsman, he was careful to take off chips of paint and clean and vacuum up as thoroughly as he could. This was still an old house and he never was sure about the paint. He never used harsh chemicals to peel the paint so as not to damage the wood. When he got to the wood he used various grades of sandpaper to smooth it. Using coarser grades at first, he methodically worked his way to finer and finer grades of paper. He would rub back and forth until he could feel the heat of the friction in his fingertips. He didn't use a sanding block or power sander because he wanted to feel the contour of the shape of the wood as he smoothed it. Sometimes, Delta would sit there and inhale the smell of the oak, that woody smell.

He was about to the point where he was finished for the evening and knew she was becoming more impatient.

"Daddy, you promised to take me trick or treating when it got dark enough."

He can't resist teasing her a bit. "I don't know it's kind of cold."

"But daddy, my friends are looking for me and all the good candy will be gone."

"Why go to all that trouble when your mother has a big bowl of candy bars by the door?"

"Mom!" She turns and yells back down the stairs and her voice carries to the hallway.

From the hallway, Doris comes gliding in to bottom of the stairs, wiping her hands on a dish towel.

"Oh, come on David! Quit teasing the girl. Really sometimes I wonder if I have two kids." Doris says huffily.

At that remark, a strange expression overtakes David and he throws down his sandpaper and bounds down the stairs like a charging bull, two stairs at a time. He is upon Doris before she can move a step. He wraps his left arm tightly around her shoulders and pulls her close to him while his other hand slinks down behind her. She lets out a sudden breath at the abruptness of his action, her mouth parts to say something as her eyes open wide. She knows what's coming next and knows there is nothing she can do to stop it.

"David, don't, Delta is right there." She motions with her head toward Delta sitting at the top of the stairs.

He smiles thinly at Doris and with his right hand he reaches down and not so discreetly pinches Doris bottom and plants a big kiss on Doris's lips.

"OOOhh, gross!" A voice from the top of the stairs intones.

"I can remember when you liked to play games like a kid." He whispers to Doris. "Ands some of those games are still illegal in a few states."

She pulls away from him a bit flushed and with a shadow of a smile on her face.

"Well just stop teasing her take your daughter out. And be careful. Don't forget, I want to see all the candy before she eats, and before you eat it too, David. And take an umbrella and your coats, it looks like rain."

"Yes Mom!" Both Delta and David echo as they laughingly scamper up the stairs.

Evening Three

Chapter 1

The wipers scraped across the windshield. They needed to be replaced; the rubber was separating at the end of the arm where they slide across the bottom of the glass leaving an area shaped like a crescent moon on the windshield. David used to clean the blades with alcohol and was going to replace them. Most of the water was slapped aside so the two occupants could see out of the car. There was not much to see beyond the two beams of light, the occasional headlights of an on coming car, creating a temporary halo rushing toward them.

Doris was driving. Her hands at ten and two on the steering wheel, staring ahead but with vacant expression through the windshield as the water was wiped one way then the other. Delta sat in the back, a lap seat belt fastened around her waist. Doris had not bothered with hers. This was a night she had been dreading. She had even put off shopping for Delta's costume till the last minute despite Delta's constant reminders for the past three weeks. Finally, Doris and Delta had found something on Halloween day at the discount store and picked up some candy. The choice of costumes had been limited but they had found a rubber robot mask that seemed to satisfy Delta. Even though the mask was too big and slipped around her head, Delta insisted on it. Delta was messing around in the bag pulling out a roll of aluminum foil and a couple of small penlight flashlights.

"Hey Mom, do we have batteries?"

Shrugging off the slight highway hypnosis that a slow steady rain induces, Doris replies. "Yes honey."

47

"Just checking." She plunges her hand into the shopping bag and pulls out the mask.

"Exactly what do you plan to do here Delta?"

"Wait and see."

"Honey, don't get your hopes up, I don't know if this rain's going to let up. You and your friends may not be able to go out tonight, at least not to many houses. Who is going with you? Janie and who else?"

"Janie and Sherri."

"Maybe I should come with you."

"But Mom we are old enough to go out by ourselves."

"Get dressed when we get home and I'll call and check with the other moms."

As they pull into the driveway, the rain tapers off and stars begin to peek out from the fluffy blanket of clouds. One of the brighter stars in the sky seems to slice through the clouds and more of the stars and the moon begin to appear. Doris stops the car, sets the brake, and she and Delta open the doors and step onto the wet, slippery driveway. A shaft of light emerges from the house as a door opens and Anna, Doris's mother, steps out onto the stoop.

"Delta, one of your little friends called, and said they would be by the house in a few minutes to go trick or treating."

"All right! I better get into my costume."

Delta runs into the house.

"Honey, I know this day is difficult. How is Delta dealing with it?" Anna asks.

"Fine I suppose. I mean she hasn't cried. Maybe she's all cried out. When we got the costume, I guess you could call it, she did ask me if I thought dad would like the costume. And for a moment, I said yes, it was as if for that split second he was here. I just wasn't thinking. Sometimes, when I'm distracted with work, I forget. No, that's not quite it. It's more like, I don't know, it's hard to describe. I guess it's like when we went camping and he would go on a long hike. Even though he wasn't with me at that moment, I knew he was still with me, I could just feel he was there even though he was miles away and over the foot hills.

"How are you dealing with it?"

"Fine. Mom it's okay. Not a day I look forward to."

"It has been a year since David died." Anna says to her.

"Delta does concern me. I mean Delta doesn't seem to know that this was the day, that David . . ."

"She's young, resilient. Kids deal with things differently, to her it's just Halloween, at her age, she doesn't relate to dates like adults."

"I'm just afraid she is forgetting David."

"She won't Doris."

"I just wish I knew she was okay, mom."

"Doris, I wish I could tell you that but all I know is that you just have to love her and help her along."

"Well, that makes me feel better considering I'm practically abandoning her to do inventory tonight."

"She won't even miss you."

"Great that makes me feel even better, Mom." Doris says with a mock sarcastic tone.

"You know what I mean." Anna says with mock seriousness but her next statement turns serious. "Doris, I'm more worried about you. You spend most of your time at the store, I know you don't sleep well, and you don't eat enough to a feed a pigeon. And are you smoking again?"

Before Doris can answer, a thumping sound comes from the stairs as Delta comes running down the stairs and into the hallway where Doris and Anna are talking.

"Look at my outfit." Delta beams. She is wrapped in tinfoil, around her legs, arms, and chest with two flashlights taped to her shoulders. She holds her mask in her hand and the empty shopping bag in the other.

"That's very creative, honey." Anna says uncertainly.

"I think it's cute. Now I want you home in one hour and don't go out from our block. Grammy is going to be strict on this, understand." Doris looks at Delta then at Anna.

"Of course." Anna replies.

"Yes Mom."

Is Janie's big sister going with you?"

"Yes, Mom."

"Okay. Well I have to work tonight. So be good." Doris carefully kisses Delta to avoid crinkling the aluminum foil.

Delta, full of energy, fiddles with her costume, making an adjustment here and there. Doris takes a bag with the candy into the kitchen and places it on the table, and drapes her rain coat over a kitchen chair. She takes big plastic bowl from the cupboard under the counter. She places the bowl on the kitchen table and pulls several bags of candy from the larger grocery bag. She rips open the smaller candy bags and dumps them into the bowl. One bag after another. A whiff of chocolate and peanut butter comes up from the bowl as she mixes it together like a chocolate salad. Unable to resist she opens one of the small bars and pops it into her mouth and she sticks a couple of bars in her rain coat for later. She hovers over the bowl, considering opening another chocolate bar. Tears begin to form in her eyes. She promptly wipes her eyes with the back of her hand, takes a deep breath, and grasps the big bowl with both hands and carries it out of the kitchen and places it on a table by the front door.

Just as the bowl contacts the table, the doorbell rings. Doris is startled just a little. Delta stops adjusting her costume and with a crinkling sound, she rushes to get to the front door. She opens the door without asking who it is or looking out the window. Standing at the door is a teenage girl, long stringy hair surrounding a partially broken out but not serious acne. Not uncommon for teenagers at this time of year with the flowing and available chocolate.

The teen has tried to cover up the acne with a little make up, at least she had the good taste not to plaster it on. After running her hand through her hair to brush it away from her face, she sticks both hands into her denim jacket, over a sweater that is tucked into to her hip hugging jeans. She glances at Delta and says in that universal, exasperated teenage tone that drips disdain for everyone and everything.

"Are you ready yet, Delta? My sister is waiting over at our house. She wants you to see her costume in the light before it gets messed up."

"You bet!" Delta replies with an ecstatic yelp that is the opposite of the teenage girl's mood.

"Let's go, I haven't got all night."

"Mom, Maureen's here. I'm going with Janie and the girls now."

"Wait, just wait." Doris comes into the hallway and over to Delta. "Now be careful, watch both ways crossing the street, and I want you home in an hour."

"Sure Mom." Delta says, a bit of the teen voice already creeping into her voice.

"Now you behave yourself, don't go past Wood street, don't eat candy unless it's wrapped and I have checked it."

"I know Mom."

"Okay then." She leans over to kiss Delta as the girl skips out the door. "Thanks Maureen." The teen replies with a grunt.

"See you later, Mom." Leaving the door open, she bounds down the front step and into the night, Maureen following her.

"Oh, to be young again." Anna huffs as she closes the front door. "She will be fine. But I know it's hard letting go, always seems they get a bit farther away."

"I know."

"The stories I could tell about you, kid."

"Please don't"

"Now you know I have to." They both start to giggle.

"One day I found you on the floor of your room when I knew I had you in the crib. I thought your dad took you out of your crib and wasn't watching you. I gave him a good talking to. Poor man didn't know what I was talking about. Then I put you back in the crib and before I could even turn around to leave, you reached up, grabbed the top rail and flipped yourself right out. You were only six months old when you lifted yourself up and over, and fell out of your crib without so much as a whimper. Never saw such a thing. Oh, you had quite the appetite. We couldn't keep you in diapers. I remember the night I left you with your daddy and the first time he saw one of your exploding poopie diapers. You were like one of those clay toys where you squeeze the crank and the clay pushes out. Except it was dirty yellow and the smell was like a trash dump in August. Your poor father, between me yelling at him and your stinky diapers."

"I guess I was quite a handful."

"Still are." The laughter of the evening carries Anna and Doris back to a time when Anna worried about Doris, the way Doris worries about Delta. As a child gets older, a mother feels like they can protect their child less and less. The mother feels more and more helpless. When a child is younger, a mother thinks they can protect children from the obvious dangers of looking both ways before crossing the street but the older they get the more danger there seems to be. The fears that a mother feels for her children, the worry that wakes a mother in the middle of the night, is always there. The knowledge that even though a mother may know best, your child may not, and you can't protect them constantly. This is both the blessing and the curse of being a mother.

"Okay, mom. I've got to get to the store." Doris says.

"You be careful too." Anna tells Doris. She grabs her coat from the chair and then heads to the front door.

Chapter 2

The three girls, Delta and her girlfriends Janie and Sherri were on their first Halloween without parents. It was the first time their parents had not accompanied them on this little October quest. The fathers had a great time accompanying the small children, it even gave some of the dads an opportunity to dress up. Of course the mothers enjoyed it as well but more along the lines of planning and dressing their children, particularly the little girls. But as the kids got older they also became more independent, wanting their dad to stay behind the tree, how different from the first Halloween when the children wanted daddy to hold their hand and walk them to the door. A boy or girl might or might not ring the bell and utter a squeaky "trick or treat" but as the years rolled by, the children became bolder and bolder. And the poor mothers, after a while they best they could hope for was a consultation on the costumes, particularly from the girls. Delta had planned and dressed herself in the robot outfit, the tinfoil she wrapped around her body crinkling every time she lifts her mask up to talk to the other girls. Janie is dressed up as a princess and Sherri in a ballerina costume. The two of them are full of compliments for each others costumes but pointedly reserve any verbal comments other than mutual eye ball rolls as they consider Delta's costume.

Their parents had told them to stay in the neighborhood and to be polite. Maureen quickly lost interest in her job when she spotted some of her friends. After a few houses the girls were out of Maureen's sight. The girls quickly filled up their bags and Sherri and Delta where wondering where to go next. However, Janie pulls out a carton of eggs from her bag.

"I've been saving these for a week, out in the storage shed in the back of our house, just like my brother used to do."

"What are you going to do with those?" Delta asks.

"Yeh, we are going to egg Mrs. McAllister's house." Sherri blurts out gleefully.

She points to one of the lighted houses at the end of the block. Mrs. McAllister is their elementary school teacher. Sherri and Janie don't have the best relationship with her, since their teacher pushes them to apply themselves, which to a little girl seems like meanness. Add to it Janie's big brother, always ready to instigate some mischief using other people including his sister.

"You will get in trouble. Besides she's not so mean." Delta says.

"She will never catch us. We stand at the street and chuck a couple of eggs and run." Sherri tells her the plan.

"I can't throw very far." Janie reminds her.

"All right we will stand in the front yard."

"Okay."

Delta scuffles along, slowing her pace. "I'm not doing it."

"There's nothing to be scared of." Sherri tells her.

"I'm not scared." Delta replies.

"But she is so mean to us in class." Janie reminds her, referring to the writing, reading, and math they are assigned. She thinks that she should be able to drop whatever she is doing and play, like at home or if she gets hungry, go get a snack, just like at home, and if she gets impatient then she should be mollified, just like at home. However, as Mrs. McAllister reminds Janie, this is school not home.

"I just don't want to do it."

"Oh, be a baby then. That means more eggs for us." Coos Sherri mockingly. Both girls swish away in their costumes. The two girls have three eggs each, juggling them in their small hands with their trick or treat bags on their wrists. Janie drops one of the eggs splatter on the side walk, spitting drops of thick putrid yellowish goo on the bottom of their skirts.

"Ewww! That stinks!" Janie and Sherri say in almost unison.

Egging houses could be considered a rite of passage for children, after all it's been a part of the youth/adult dynamic for years since the Halloween custom or holiday or what ever you choose to call it was conceived. A treat or you get a trick is just extortion in a more juvenile form. Perhaps for a child it is a way to express their emotions, an implied socially acceptable way to rage at authority. Janie and Sherri have assumed that this has never been done before, egging a teacher's house, when in fact many teachers expect it to some degree and have a subconscious watchfulness for it.

A whisper of a cool wind but no rain grazed the girls as they separated and the light grew dimmer and dimmer from the street lights that bathed everything in a peculiar blue green luminescence mixed with the white porch lights of the houses. The other two girls were preparing to execute their trick. They both continue down the street giggling, leaving Delta at a corner of the neighborhood. The first wave of trick or treaters, the young kids with their parents had already been through this part. Parents, some dressed in costumes themselves, with little two year olds just old enough to walk and run made all the more difficult by long costumes and masks covering their faces, made their mastery of gravity all the more tenuous. But the parents were there to catch them and keep them safe.

Delta walked along slowly, her contrived robot cyborg costume crinkling. She turns off the flashlight on her shoulder and slowly peels the foil and crumples it and throws it into her trick or treat bag. Suddenly, tonight does not seem fun. She continues to walk.

A mist creeps in as Delta walks down a street of her neighborhood, checking out which houses have porch lights on and which houses are decorated. She rings a few doorbells since she still has her mask but after collecting a bag full and eating some candy, she doesn't bother going to any more houses. After a while, she becomes interested in the houses. Most have some decorations. Some have simple cardboard skeletons or monsters or signs but there are more elaborate ones. One house has the porch covered in spider webs of cotton batting pulled apart and large plastic spiders all over it. Another house has a scarecrow sitting on the porch. On the garage of one house, they have set up spot light that cast shadows of ghosts on the garage door.

Before she knows it, she is all the way down the street and out of their immediate neighborhood. By this time she is getting hungry and decides to get more candy. She walks up to a house that is lit but has no decorations. Delta rings the doorbell and a middle aged woman answers the door, cheerfully even though it is getting late.

"Well, what happened to your costume, dear?"

Delta blanks for a second. "Oh, I got tired and took it off."

"No matter, here you go dear." The woman puts a candy caramel apple into her bag wrapped in foil.

"Thanks."

Delta walks back down the path to the sidewalk and turns and heads for home. She reaches into her bag and pulls out the apple.

She hears occasional giggles and screeches of the older kids and teenagers out late. She hears the faster steps of some teens as they rush by her trailing some rolls of toilet paper. She continues along and seems to hear steps behind her; she glances back but senses only shadows. She quickens her pace a bit. Even though it is a safe neighborhood, something in her feels the cold and darkness, it is not just the coldness on her skin or the absence of light for her eyes to detect, it is a feeling of loneliness she feels in the night. She crosses the street, to a house with hedges as tall as she is; she imagines that someone could hide in there and grab her. All sorts of thoughts fly through her mind. She hears a something like a scraping on the concrete sidewalk and glances back to catch a glimpse of a moving shadow.

"Who is that!" She tries to say without fear in her voice but the tremor is unmistakable.

A figure leaps from the shadows behind her.

"You're missing all the fun!" Sherri yells at her as she and Janie streak past her, trying to catch up with the older kids that had passed by. Apparently there had been other vandals out that night.

"So what." She says to herself. So what if her friends abandoned her. She pulls out the candy apple and carefully peels off the wrapper and savors the smell of the caramel. Her mother told her not to eat any unwrapped candy including home made treats but Delta likes apples. She holds it carefully by the stick, so as not to get the sticky caramel on her fingers. Suddenly, the apple flies out of her hand. She screams in surprise. Then screams again when she sees a tall figure emerge out of the shadows. She thinks about running but somehow her legs just aren't moving. As she stands there, the figure moves close to her. The tall figure leans over and in a deep masculine voice, his face so close, she can feel a warm breath against her cheek. He tells her, "Don't eat the apples from that house, and don't let anyone else eat the apples. Get home and tell your mother."

She closes her eyes for a moment, when she opens them the figure is gone. She sprints home.

Evening Four

Chapter 1

This year was going to be a very different Halloween. There was more parental supervision than usual. That included Janie and Sherri in particular. Both of the girls got in considerable trouble when their parents found out what they had been up to. Mrs. McAllister had been very understanding. The two girls did spend a weekend cleaning up the mess and returned every weekend after that for a month to pick up in her yard. In addition they were grounded and had no television or after school playing until December. Delta didn't get in trouble but neither did she tell on the girls. To Sherri and Janie's credit they said that Delta wasn't with them. But it was still a night Sherri and Janie and in particular, Delta would never forget.

Sherri and Janie were still out when the first porch lights were being turned off. They were already in trouble, and Maureen for missing curfew set by their parents. They had crept into the front yard of their teacher's house and attempted to throw the eggs. The eggs had spoiled and rotted from the inside. The shell had softened. So when they tried to throw the first egg, Sherri raised it above her head and just as she was about to release it, she accidentally squished it. The egg white and yolk oozed between her fingers and ran down her arm and part of the mess it fell into her hair. If she hadn't been afraid of being caught she would have squealed in disgust. Janie was a bit more successful. She took the carton from Sherri and actually got three eggs out of the carton and managed to hit the front of the house, just above the front door. The eggs hit silently and slid down the side of the house. Before they started their prank, the girls would dive into the bushes lining the front of the house when they heard someone approaching up the sidewalk. So they did the same thing when they heard some trick or treaters approaching. Unfortunately, Janie tripped on a root as they dived into the bushes and Sherri fell on top of her and Janie landed on the remaining eggs. The entire front of their costumes was a gooey, smelly mess.

The girls were trying to clean the goop out of their hair and off their costumes. They were so engrossed in trying to clean up they didn't notice the two approaching figures, two beams of light emanated from the two figures, beams of light crisscrossing the sidewalk, the beams found the two girls. After a couple of clicks, the flashlights were turned off, and it gradually became apparent as the girl's eyes adjusted after the brightness of the flash lights that the two people were their fathers and they were not happy. Both men looked from the girls to the McAllister's house and the explanations from the girls were to no avail. They tried to blame it on teenagers but the goo stuck in their hair and the reek of rotten eggs on their costumes made their attempts at excuses a futile effort in the face of such evidence.

At Delta's grandparent's house, now her and her mother's home, tragic Sherri's and Janie's adventure paled in comparison to Delta's experiences last year.

"Delta, come on downstairs honey." Her mother called upstairs, one foot on the first step and fingers clasped on the hand rail. Anna is standing behind Doris with her coat on.

"Hey, Mom." Delta replied. "It's almost dark out, can we go now?"

"Let's wait a bit longer."

After last year, her mother is accompanying her as are most parents. After the nightmare of last year's Halloween, many parents had considered canceling the whole thing.

Delta jumps from step to step down to the bottom, her long dress still swaying as she comes to a stop in front of her mother. Doris had found the pink and white dress at a second hand store and tied on a few ribbons and bows to make it more like a princess's gown. Delta had been ecstatic since she was now enamored of princesses this year. Doris figured Delta could get some more wear out of the dress for church and other occasions.

Doris puts her hand on top of Delta's head, she is growing so fast. It seems like Delta was just in diapers, sometimes you wonder who this little person is. Every morning it's like meeting a slightly new person as they grow and mature and learn but they are still the same little child from yesterday and the day before. While at the same time it seems you have known them forever, you can't really recall what your life was before they arrived. You think you were carefree, no troubles and free to do as you please. Why, if you wanted to quit your job and head to China, you certainly could have. Of course, you didn't. Whether most people care to admit or not, there is this little voice in the back of their minds that is whispering; I sure wish I had a little girl or wouldn't it be great to have a little boy. With children, time does not flow like a gentle river, time roars past like a flood. If you're lucky you get little snapshots of time as their lives rush past you. A birthday, a Halloween, a Christmas and then you start over again, always looking at the pictures from year to year, incredulous at how they have changed.

"I can remember when we couldn't get you in a dress. Your grandma would buy some cute little dress for you and you would squeal to get out of it."

"Okay kid, lets eat a quick dinner then we can go out." Doris looks at Delta in her princess costume, the white stocking and pink bows with tennis shoes. "Wait a minute I gotta get a picture."

"Mom." Exasperated Delta replies. "That was when I was little, mommy."

"I remember your costume from last year; you were a super hero in tin foil. You look so pretty this year." Anna says.

"Oh, Grammy there are pictures of me in dresses."

"There were quick shots. Let me tell you girl. The only person that could get you in a skirt was your daddy." Anna mentions. "Anyway, I've got to go and meet you grandfather down at the hardware store. You and your mom have fun." Anna buttons her coat then squeezes Doris's shoulder with her hand. A slice of cool air slides into the front hallway from outside as Anna opens then closes the door as she leaves.

After a year it has become easier to talk about her dad, it is almost like he is still around. It some strange way it is like he is always at work or on a trip but is still a part of their lives. The doorbell rings and Delta walks over to open the door.

"Trick or treat!" Melba shrieks, Deltas other grandparent and her father's mother.

"Hey grandma." Delta leans over and gives her grandma a hug as she comes inside.

"Thanks for coming over Melba. I set out a big bowl of candy." She points to the table near the front door. We should be gone, what fifteen minutes?" She teases Delta. "After we get back, I need to run to the hardware store and get the accounting books updated with mom and dad."

"Delta, how does a ham sandwich sound?" Doris asks.

"Yummy Mom." She streaks into the kitchen leaving Doris, Melba, and Anna in the living room.

"Are you really going to let her have any candy this year." Melba sounds concerned as she removes her coat.

With a little hesitation, Doris replies, "Sure, I think it's safe. We are only going to houses we know, eat only wrapped candy. The hospital will even x-ray candy if you're that concerned. Wouldn't have really helped with last year."

"It could've been a lot worse." Doris then adds. "Really if it hadn't been for Delta, I still don't know how she figured it out."

"True, but how could someone give away those caramel apples, without knowing they were dangerous?"

"Well they determined it wasn't intentional." Doris answers Melba. "That poor woman just didn't know."

"Yeh, she got some bad apples from a small farm upstate. They were using some pesticide they shouldn't have been using. Melba adds. "But still, she should have washed them . . ."

"It wouldn't have changed anything; the poison was soaked through the apple just not on the skin, that's why they don't use that stuff." Doris injects.

"Just fortunate that nobody else used those apples for Halloween and that Delta noticed before anyone got to sick."

"I know it was amazing how she noticed the apples were poison. I still can't figure it out, how she did that. Was it the smell?" Melba shakes her head. "Kids notice a lot of things, that adults miss, I suppose. Different perspective. To us it's an apple; to kids it's a treat."

"True." Doris agrees.

"I should have brought my scrap book. I put all the articles from the paper in it. I even got a picture of the mayor shaking hands with Delta at his office for saving other kids." Melba says.

"It still concerns me though that something like that could happen." Doris ponders.

"Should dear." Melba says. "That sort of thing always has the possibility of happening."

"I do feel sorry for that poor woman." Doris says.

"You mean the one that gave out the apples? Why? They should have run her out on a rail." Melba says.

"That's almost what happened." Doris says. "People were just horrid to her. She had to move."

"What concerns me is the man she talked about." Melba interjects.

"Delta said that a man told her about the apples." Doris says. "They never found any man around that might have known about those apples."

"For all we know it could have been a farm hand or somebody that worked at the orchard." Melba says.

"Then why travel down here and warn one kid? Why not call the police? Strange, very strange."

"Maybe she just imagined him, it could have been Delta's way of figuring it out. Maybe she smelled something not right on the apple. She is smart, she might have sensed something then maybe imagined it was an adult that warned her. Little kids think different."

"Suppose, I guess." Doris says.

"Or maybe . . ." Melba starts to reply.

"Maybe, what?" Doris asks.

"Maybe, she is a bit psychic." Melba says.

"What?"

"Delta could be psychic. It was on that talk show, they had a psychic on there. Could tell things about people he never met before. It was amazing. Just like it was amazing how Delta knew something was wrong. Sometimes children pick up on things."

"Melba, she might have sensed something wasn't quite right but please don't get ridiculous and don't put that nonsense in Delta's head either."

"Okay, okay, I guess it's safer to go out this year. I don't know, we certainly thought it was safe last year . . ." Melba says. "Why go at all?"

An exasperated Doris says. "What and risk a coup in the family? Delta would have a fit and I wouldn't blame her."

Delta comes trotting out of the kitchen, wiping off a milk mustache with the back of her hand.

"Hey Mom are you ready to go?" Delta asks as the phone rings.

"Just a minute honey." Doris says as she walks over to the ringing phone and answers it.

"You look beautiful, Delta." Melba says as Doris whispers urgently into the telephone receiver.

"I really like this costume, all pink and very feminine, with a . . . , what do you call those skirts?"

"A skirt, grandma."

"Of course."

In the background, Doris hangs up the phone, the crows feet at the corners of her eyes, clinching just a little tighter as she says to Delta, "Honey, that was your grandpa, he and grandma need me, the shipment of power tools, the company wants cash on delivery. I need to go in to the office and pull some documents together. I don't like doing this but the delivery is tomorrow. I'm sorry."

"That means she can't go out?" Melba asks. "I mean I was planning to stay here and give out candy, but what if I took her?"

Delta is also ready with an alternative. "What about Sherri's Mom? I could go with them."

"I know honey." Doris replies to Delta. How do you explain to a young child all your fears for them, some irrational and some rational. How do you explain your fears and puncture the bubble of innocence that children will lose anyway. Balancing between scarring them and preparing them is such a thin line. Trust nobody, suspect everyone, is that the idea to instill in children? Is it worth it if it protects them? Is that a way to grow up? Is that the extreme that a parent must go to keep children safe? If so maybe Doris should just bolt the doors right now and lock them all in. Hasn't she felt like doing that a million times over the past year?

Instead she says to Delta, "All right, you can be with your friends and have fun but not too much fun. But you be careful. I'm walking you over to Sherri's house and make sure there is adult supervision this year."

"Okay Mommy." She giggles as she tugs at her dress.

They head toward the door; Melba comes striding toward them before they can leave.

"You can't go out like that." She tells Doris and Delta. "Here I got your coats. Go out and have a good time. I'll stay here and give out candy." She says smiling. "Don't leave without some candy." She grabs some candy from the bowl on the table by the door; and tosses some chocolate bars to Doris. Catching the candy, Doris smiles a thank you to Melba.

Chapter 2

Slipping her coat on, a garment she has had for ten years, frayed but warm, Doris opens the door, makes sure Delta has her candy bag, they walk down the street to meet Delta's friend Sherri at her house. Delta trots down the sidewalk, her breath escaping in small puffs as the cool October air of the early evening condenses her breath. Doris follows briskly behind. This was to be the first time she had taken Delta trick or treating, David had always done it before except for last year. The laughter of the children mixed with roars as someone tried to scare someone who squeals in mock horror. The smell of burning wood in fireplaces as most people are having fires for the first time this season, mixed with the smells of dinners left half finished. Bright colorful costumes are everywhere as children scramble around, giddy on a sugar rush already.

They come to Sherri's house. They walk up the steps and to the door, Doris can hear voices inside. An argument apparently, Doris can hear Sherri and her mother arguing. Doris is hesitant to go to the door but the voices are quiet after a few moments. There is little doubt as to who won the argument. So she knocks on the door.

Mrs. Ales opens the door, flooding the darkness with a wedge of bright light. Behind Mrs. Ales is Sherri and Jill, Sherri's other teenage sister, standing with their arms crossed and their chins stuck to their chest. Apparently, neither is very excited by each other's company this evening.

Doris nods in greeting to Mrs. Ales. "Sorry about the late notice but can Delta go with Sherri and your husband tonight?"

"Oh, well, Tom is sick tonight. We were just having a discussion about that. Jill has agreed to take Sherri out this year so we don't have any incidents"

Doris sighs. She wanted an adult with Delta tonight. But she doesn't want to disappoint Delta and it really is a safe neighboorhood. "I really appreciate you taking Delta out around the neighborhood Jill." Doris says.

At first Jill doesn't reply until her mother shoots a dagger of a stare at her and then she replies, "You're welcome." Said with clenched jaw and staring at the floor.

Doris and Mrs. Ales share a sly smile.

Sherri comes running up in her princess costume and shoots by everyone and grabs Delta's hand as they both head outside. "I guess Sherri is ready too." Mrs. Ales says.

"Jill, better catch up with them."

Jill slips past Doris and Mrs. Ales without a word and she's out the door. She walks a few steps and yells at Delta and Sherri. "Stop right now!"

Delta and Sherri reluctantly wait for Jill to catch up. Jill follows along as Delta and Sherri eagerly run from house to house. Jill trudges up to them at the sidewalk for another house. Jill is going to yell at Delta and Sherri to slow down and how she is not their babysitter when a teenage boy walks up.

"Hey." He says to Jill.

"Hey." She replies, smiling a little.

"You're in my Algebra class, right?" He knows that she is.

"Yeah. I sit by the window so I can look outside." Jill says.

"Smart. Class is so boring."

"Totally." She replies.

"What you up to?" He asks.

"Taking my little sister and her dorky friend trick or treating."

"Really."

"What are you up to tonight?"

"Just wandering around, checking things out." Which was sort of true. He had been walking up and down the street in front of Jill's house for half an hour waiting for her to come out. He had been following behind them, wanting to talk to Jill.

"Cool."

"I'm heading over to the burger place, want to go along?" He tries to ask nonchalantly as his voice breaks a little.

Jill hesitates as she looks over at Sherri and Delta but then gets a smile on her face. "Sure, just a minute."

Jill walks over to the two girls and tells them, "I'm going to let you two losers go trick or treating by yourselves. So if mom asks, I was with you guys the whole night. If she finds out otherwise, I'll beat the snot out of you. Got it?"

They both nod. They were happy to see Jill go.

Sherri and Delta run across the street. Cars, for the most part, move at a snails pace, their headlights illuminating little swathes of the eerie scene of kids in weird costumes yelling and running around in unrestrained joy, hyped up on sugar. They turn up the next sidewalk and run up to the door and ring the bell.

They come to the next house and Sherri stops.

"Oh my gosh! This is Tub's house!" She squeals.

"So?" Delta replies. She does not have the same fascination with boys that Sherri has recently obtained, and that Sherri apparently shares with her sister Jill.

Just as they are walking up to the house, Tub and some of his friends come sprinting up the grass, they are a few months older than Delta and Sherri. But Sherri's on the fast track to maturity. She has overheard her sister talking to her friends and even read some of Jill's magazines and romance novels that Jill hides under her bed.

"Hi, Tub." Sherri says.

"Been out trick or treating?" He asks.

"Yeah."

Delta tries to drag her friend away by trying to nudge her to the next house but Sherri is having none of that. While Sherri carries on her rather limited conversation with Tub, Delta slips to the next house.

After a few houses, most of the fun has gone out of the night. Her friend became preoccupied. She realizes in all the mass of people, children running and parents trying to keep up, she doesn't know where her house is. It is getting really dark. The street lights are all on, in addition to the inside and outside lights of the houses. The amalgamation of all those lights creates a pale glow throughout the neighborhood. It also casts confusing shadows. As some children run by, they cast several dim shadows that point in all directions. Looking at her own shadow, she is able to make it dimmer or brighter by getting closer to the next street light. Dim, dimmer till it's almost gone until the next street light casts a shadow and it becomes stronger and stronger till she is directly under it. That's why it probably startles her more than anything else when the man speaks. She looks up from the sidewalk at the direction of the voice and the man who said it. Then she looks up and sees a man standing there under the same street light.

"Delta, it's me."

Delta looks at the man. She is unsure at first but the voice is so familiar.

"I know . . ." She hesitates.

"Do you remember me?"

She knows the voice, the same voice that warned her about the poison apple last year. More than that, the voice was even more familiar and comforting to her. Part of her wanted to say, yes I know that voice. She wanted to wrap her arms around that voice and hug it.

"Honey, it's me."

Perhaps it is easier for children to grasp what seems impossible but suddenly her mind and heart agreed on whose voice this is.

"Daddy!" She screams to the figure as she wraps her arms around the figure, her heart full of joy but her mind was wondering what was going on. Her arms find him, warm and smelling musky from work like he used to. He wrapped his arms around her, like she remembered, half lifting her up.

"I missed you so much. We're so sad, especially mommy."

His mind was whirling with thoughts of his family; images, sounds, and feelings that seemed familiar but he couldn't focus them, it was a mental mist that he tried to push through. The images were of his wife and daughter, very familiar yet the same time remote. A birthday party, the smell of candles burning on a dark, chocolate cake, even the taste of it seemed to be on his tongue. Lots of children running around, playing some game, it's pin the tail on the donkey. So much fun, so much happiness. It almost overwhelms him, feelings that are familiar but seems so long since he has felt these emotions, it was like waking from a deep slumber, everything is groggy and disorienting until slowly the world comes into focus. But at this time, his thoughts, memories are all focused on Delta, his little girl; so long since he has seen her, felt her presence so near to him, But he also feels a tug pulling him away from her, it is a feeling he wants to distance himself from but knows he can't. Now that he is here with her, the coldness that gripped his heart is relieved, but not entirely gone.

Delta is so happy to see her father. And has no doubt that this is her father even though her mother has told her that he died. This does confuse Delta but here is her father, standing in front of her, hugging her. So this is what she believes. That is the innocence of children. The ability to suspend disbelief is something we will lose as we grow older but secretly hope that someday we will regain the ability to see everything in the fresh way we first saw everything in the world. This is the wonder with which Delta sees her father. He is with her tonight. The thought that he might have abandoned them doesn't occur to her. She doesn't bother with the possibilities. It's possible he got tired of the family responsibility and ran off. It's possible he saw his chance for his family to cash in on his life insurance. It's possible he is a ghost. It doesn't matter to her because she is with her daddy, and it doesn't matter whether it is possible or not. To her, all the possibilities seem equally possible. After all what are the odds that anyone would be born on this planet that just happens to be far enough from its sun for life to survive? What is the probability that people would even exist on a planet conducive to life in a universe so vast and so lacking apparently in life? Just a coincidence, the natural capriciousness of existence? Is life just an accident? Odds so long they can't even be realistically calculated? Are people just the unplanned pregnancy of the universe? And if so, is it then any more unlikely that Delta's father should be standing with her? There are many variables and people make assumptions that are sometimes correct and sometimes not. There are many possibilities. Some are more probable than others. But to a little girl, all the possibilities and probabilities are not relevant or of much interest to her. All she knows is that her daddy is with her.

David reaches out his hand to Delta and then hugs her close to him. It pops into his mind, how she has grown. She doesn't move away from him or his touch, as his fingers slightly touch the top of her head and his fingers play lightly with a few strands of her rich hair. Warm now, he just realizes how cold he felt before. In her presence, it's like warming your hands and face at a gentle fire in fire place.

"Oh, daddy, I've missed you so much!" His daughter tells him. He looks down at her, at her gap toothed smile and it is the most beautiful thing he has ever seen.

"Honey, I'm sorry, so sorry." Though he can't recall quite what he is sorry for, not being there for her? Or for his daughter and for her mother. His eyes become heavy and damp as he begins to remember Doris.

"Where have you been?" She says that in a typical child; petulant tone.

He thinks for a moment and decides to tell her the truth. "I can't tell you honey."

"But Mommy has been so sad, she cries sometimes when she's in her room, she thinks I don't know but I do."

"She does? David doesn't know what to say. He wants to run back to their house, to Delta and her mother but he can't quite see a way back, if he could, he would run, burst through the front door with Delta in his arms, find his wife and stay with them forever. But he can't.

"Daddy are you coming home?"

He needs to delay answering the question because he has no answer for her. "Honey, its Halloween isn't it? So why don't we go trick or treating?"

"Okay daddy!" The idea of collecting candy with her daddy is irresistible to a little girl.

They walk down the street and blend in with all the other children and their parents as they walk around the neighborhood. David nods to other dads out with their kids. Occasionally, as David and another dad are waiting for their children to ring doorbells at the same house, they will make small talk. Usually about the end of the baseball season and start of the football season, problems with cars or the weather is so unpredictable. If it wasn't for weather, cars and sports; men would have nothing to talk about. David and Delta are having fun as they trick or treat on Halloween. Delta's bag of treats is near to bursting as she holds the bag tightly in one hand and her father's hand even tighter in her other hand.

Later in the evening as their night is winding down they come to a house that is dark and no porch light on. Two large oak trees stand in the front yard gently swaying to a cool night breeze. Delta and her dad hear a rustling in the bushes to their left and then foot steps behind them.

"Don't sweat it, man." A low voice says and then the same person in a slightly higher pitched voice. "It's a kid and her brother." Two males step from the bushes and onto the sidewalk.

David looks them over and asks them. "What are you up to, hiding in the bushes?"

"What you think?" The male with the up and down pitched voice responds. "We're TPing this house."

The other male, also a teenager, walks up carrying a pillow case full of toilet paper and stands beside his friend. Even in the dim light his face is greasy with red pimples cratering his face.

"Why are you toilet papering this house?" David asks.

"Why not? They're not giving out any more candy. They're asking for somebody to prank em." The one holding the pillow case responds, reaching into the pillowcase and pulling out a roll. David looks at the roll. He shakes his head in disappointment.

David looks at him for a moment and says. "You're not using that paper to TP this house."

The two boys look at each other then back to David. "Give me that bag." They hesitate to do what David tells them. David reaches for it and the teen reluctantly lifts his arm and David snatches it from him.

David reaches into the bag pulling out one then two rolls and keeps them. Looking into the bag he rummages around, there are four rolls left; he then pulls out a roll tosses one to the high/low pitched voice teen and then one to the teen with acne.

"Okay guys, the thing to remember is always go with high quality, two ply paper. That cheap, single ply stuff I just tossed out will just shred and come apart in the tree. Rule of thumb, if it ain't good for wiping your butt, it ain't good for TPing."

The two teens grin and nod their heads. David nods back, motions to Delta with his hand and they continue walking down the sidewalk. Delta whispers up to him, "My dad is smart."

"Darn right." They stop and look back. One of the boys throws the roll of toilet paper high in the air but it doesn't unfurl. Rookie mistake, you have to start the roll by pulling on the first square. The teen runs over to where the roll landed, looks at it and throws it in a high arc toward one of the trees in the yard. The roll gets stuck on a lower branch about ten feet off the ground. He looks around for help but the other teen is trying to throw his roll in the other tree but after several attempts, he hasn't hit the tree once. He has an awkward sidearm throwing motion, imagine a kangaroo with its short arms trying to throw a softball and that describes this kids throwing motion. The two teenagers finally manage to get quite a bit of paper hanging from the trees, most of it hanging almost to the ground like little white stalactites. The other teenager who stuck the toilet roll in the tree has found a six foot stick on the ground. At first he tries to poke the roll out of the tree but it's just out of reach. Then he throws the stick straight up and it hits the roll but the stick is caught in the tree. The teenager picks up the toilet roll, soggy and dirty and congratulates himself on getting it out of the tree with one throw of the stick. And hurls it back into the tree. He wonders where the limb went and looks straight up just as a little breeze blows through the tree, just enough to dislodge it. The limb slides relatively slowly, slowly enough that the teen can see it sliding down but like a rat mesmerized by a cobra, he doesn't move. The limb, the diameter of a thick broom handle, slides from the tree and hits him in the forehead. The teen starts cussing. The other teenager begins laughing and collapses to his knees in a pile of leaves. He places his right hand on the ground to lift himself up and he gets a big clump of mud all over his hand. He shakes it off and wipes it off on the back of his jeans. Suddenly he can smell something like rotten eggs except they were TPing the house not egging the house. He wipes his nose with his right hand and the smell makes him stagger. He had put his hand in a pile of dog poop. And it was all over the back of his jeans. They had no TP left. It was all in the trees so he walks over to pull a piece out of the tree. It disintegrates in his hand. As he is walking under the trees, long strips of TP hanging from the tree limbs gets stuck to the poop on his pants. He looks like a hapless bug stuck in a huge, ivory spider web. He twists and turns trying to get the TP off but just gets more entangled.

David shakes his head and mutters, "How come these two haven't been caught yet? The people in the house have got to hear them."

"They don't care." Delta replies. "The boy with the pimples lives in the house."

"Toilet papering his own house?"

"Yep. His parents don't mind. Mommy says his parents don't want him to get in trouble doing some body else's house."

"Okay, I guess things have changed since I was a kid." They continue walking. David says to Delta, "Those two numbnuts were terrible. They couldn't even hit the tree. Sorry. I told your Mom I wouldn't use that word. Those guys were terrible."

"Can you teach me to TP?"

"Well, that's a prank more for guys . . ."

"That's not what mom says."

"She talks about what pranks you can pull?"

"No silly. About girls doing stuff anything boys can do."

"Oh, well, she's right. Girls can do most of the same stuff as guys."

"So you'll teach me?"

"When you're a teenager."

As they near Delta's house the mood changes for David. But Delta assumed he was coming home. Delta was skipping along, they were nearing their house, they stopped suddenly, or more accurately David came slowly to a halt, just a ways up from the house.

"Delta, stop, please." David implores her.

"Okay daddy." She was so happy and he knew he had to tell her the one thing she didn't want to hear.

"Honey, you know, I love you." He stopped, it was so painful, a real physical pain to him.

"I want to eat my candy. I want to go home." She says wearily.

"I can't. I want to but I can't. And you can't tell your mom or anybody."

"Why not? Mommy would be so happy . . ."

He tries to think of something to tell her, some way to explain. He blurts out, "Honey, if you go around saying you saw me, they will probably arrest your mom. They could arrest your mom for fraud for collecting on my life insurance if you go telling people I'm around. I know it's hard but you can't tell anyone."

She tilts her head and asks, "What's fraud?"

He tries to think of something she will understand. So he simply tells her. "I'll come and see you when I can. But Delta, you can't tell anyone about me or I can't come around ever."

"I know."

"You do?" David is bewildered.

"Like when the dad in the story had to go away because his daughter messed up."

Perplexed he can only look at her.

"My book about the little princess. I promise daddy, I won't mess up. Just come back when you can. Promise?"

He has no reply to this but David does remember the story he would read to Delta at bedtime. 'The Little Princess of Snow Lake'. How could he forget the book that he read over and over to his daughter?

Evening Five

David covers the ground to Sherri's house in a short time; it was the house down from where his wife and daughter now live. He could not believe how little effort it took to cover the distance to the burning house. The two story colonial is spewing smoke out of the cracks in the windows and doors. He jumps up the steps in front of the house, reaches out for the door and finds that it is locked, he twists it again, a little harder, and it snaps open as he pushes into it. He knows he should fall to the floor crawl but the smoke doesn't bother him and he can sort of see though the dense opaque air, he simply navigates through the front room and directly to the kitchen where he knows he will find Sherri's father, Tom. Cutting through the smoke like a shadow on a fog bank, he comes to the swinging door to the kitchen. He pushes it open and thick black smoke rolls out the doorway, enveloping him. Crossing the threshold, he can see the man, collapsed by the kitchen sink, a pan beside him as a faucet is on full, pouring into the sink and down the drain. David can sense he is still alive. It is a combination of all his senses, all smashed together, washing over him, all the senses into one sensation. This sensation allows David to differentiate the man on the floor from the stove which is ablaze in a very intense grease fire with lots of thick smoke. David senses the environment around him but he knows there is a back door just across from the sink on the other wall. Picking up the other man and pulling him to the door leading out to the yard. Kicking it open, the door flies off its hinges and he walks out into cool night air. He carries the man down to the lawn and lays him on his back, cradling his head with his hand. Sirens and lights are blaring in the front of the house. The noise of trucks and men rushing about are in front of the house, hoses spraying water and crashing wood are heard in the front. Steps of heavy boots are coming around the house.

The first fireman in the backyard sees David and the man on the ground.

"Good job, dude!" The fireman says to David. David looks down at himself and he is dressed in yellowish leather pants and black boots. He reaches to his head and feels a fireman's helmet. "But next time wait for the rest of us before you go bursting into the house." David rises and steps back toward the fence, into the shadows of the trees lining the back of the yard. A little later, more firemen burst into the backyard.

"Get some oxygen!" The first fireman yells at the arriving firefighters as Sherri and Delta run into the backyard.

A fireman places an oxygen mask over the old man's face and soon he is coughing and wheezing but conscious.

"Dad!" Sherri runs over to him and hugs him but the man is dazed and somewhat confused.

"What happened?" He gasps, attempting to rise.

"Sir! Please lay down." The fireman tells him.

"Dad! Dad! Please . . ." Sherri yells.

"Who are you people? What is this?" The man says. The paramedics and Sherri soothes him telling him to lie still; telling him everything is going to be fine.

In the backyard, David hovers in the shadows; Delta notices him and walks over to the trees in the backyard. At first she had a hard time seeing him until he steps out to her from the shadow.

"Delta, are you okay?"

"Yes daddy." She rushes to hug him. "I wondered where you went. I thought you left already."

"Come here." David hugs Delta, comforting her.

"Daddy."

Yes, hon."

"When did you grow a mustache? She pauses and says, "Why are you dressed like a fireman?"

He takes a deep breath, "That's a very good question . . ."

Doris and Sherri's mother rush into the backyard. Sherri's mother kneels by Tom. Doris looks for Delta. At first she thought Delta was inside the house but Sherri told her they were together. She scans the yard and makes out dim shapes under the trees. She walks over to the trees to see if it is Delta. She sees Delta. Delta runs to her and they head back to the house. Doris turns back around when she thinks she catches a glimpse of someone in her peripheral vision but there's no one there.

Chapter 2

The eye itself is a magnificent sensing organ but is far from perfect. It is very fragile, the difference between seeing 20/20 and blindness is a matter of millimeters. A torn retina, a bruised cornea and blindness can be the result. Just a few cells misaligned and that's all it takes for the eye to break down. A philary duct gets clogged and glaucoma results. Sight is a sense that is so amazing and so fragile.

The eye and the way our brain processes the minute electrical impulses from the eye allows us to sense so much. But we only see a very small part of the spectrum of waves of electromagnetic energy that is actually there. The visible spectrum is small compared to the rest of the energy spectrum, if it were a mile long; we only see a fraction of it. There is such a diversity of energy that can't be seen. The brain does the 'seeing', the eye is the sensing organ. There is a test for aircraft pilots where they look at two concentric circles, one has dot and the other doesn't. So when one eye is closed you can see one circle has a dot but the other doesn't. Look with both eyes and it appears there is a dot in both circles. But your brain fills in the other dot, telling you there are dots in both circles.

Doris looked again in the shadows under the trees in the backyard. She pulled her sweater tighter around her shoulders as a chilly breeze caught up to her and she walked back onto the lawn where firemen had Sherri's father on a gurney. Sherri and her mother walk along to the ambulance.

"Momma." Delta ran over to her mother.

"Lets go home, Delta."

As their leaving the firemen that was first one the scene, yells over to another fireman, "Hey! Where's the other guy?"

"What guy?"

"The new guy. He really hustled in after the old guy."

"Don't know. He's probably over by the truck by now."

The voices trail off as Doris and Delta walk home.

Evening Six

Twirling her long dress to the disco music made her a bit dizzy, but the music was what all the other kids were listening at school. Delta as well as her friends were going as disco dancers. The costume was basically a dress and leotard with boots. Her mom had bought her the new black leather boots; none of her fiends had them yet. Doris had offered to buy her entire ensemble but Delta already had it planned. They went out shopping together although Doris had been very busy lately, but she wanted to take time to go shopping with her daughter.

"Delta are you ready? I don't hear your friends. Were they coming by here?" Her mother said from the kitchen.

"No, Mom." She said furtively. "I'm going to meet them down at the corner.

"Okay, but don't go too far, and remember, take your flashlight. Watch out for traffic." He mother says as she comes out of the kitchen. She looks at Delta and how she has grown.

"What do you think Mom? Neat, huh?"

"It certainly is." Doris looks at her daughter. If only David could see her now. What a waste, she thinks.

"I'm a disco dancer, Mom!"

"Really? I would never have guessed."

"Oh, Mom!"

"All right, go on, have fun with your friends. But be careful." She strides over to give Delta a hug which Delta wiggles away from as if she is too old but doesn't struggle that much. As soon as Doris releases her, Delta with a quick glance at her Mom, slips out the door and down the steps then along the sidewalk to the other corner. She looks back over her shoulder, her mother isn't looking and she just keeps going down the block. Night is overtaking dusk and the trick or treaters are out in force searching for the houses with the tastiest candy. She walks the streets of her neighborhood, looking for something else. For something just past childhood but short of adulthood, a twilight before the dawn of adulthood. She seeks illumination on what she believed as a child but could never believe as an adult.

"Delta." A voice calls.

She looks around, unsure in her mind of what she hears and sees, like the fairy tales children sometimes believe but wonder if their really true and are usually disappointed that they are not. But not this time. There he is, there is her father, just as he was last year.

"Daddy." She runs into his arms.

"Oh, honey." I missed you so much. Wow, you've grown!" He is sad for moment but then the excitement of the night takes hold.

"Well, I am out of elementary school, you know."

"Wow, really."

"Dad, this last year, you know I've been wondering about stuff."

"What kind of stuff?" He thinks to himself maybe this is a conversation best left to Doris, which at the next moment strikes him as hopelessly tragic.

"I've been wondering . . ."

"About what Delta!"

"About you."

"I thought we covered that?"

"I know but in school and church . . . I mean it can't be you." She reaches up to touch his face. You're here." As her hand caresses his warm cheek. "How is it possible?"

"I don't know Delta. I wish I could tell you."

They walk for awhile. "Do you want to trick or treat?" He asks.

"Not really."

"Tell me about your Mom and we can stop at some houses." He says longingly. "How is she doing?"

"Yeah Mom is doing fine. She works like really hard. She has five hardware stores now. She even says she will turn them into a chain in the state, a sort of supermarket for nails and screws and stuff I guess. They're big stores just for house stuff, hardware stuff, so anybody can come in and get anything they need to fix up their house. Anything like tools, lumber, gardening things, you name it."

"Interesting. Your mom always was a planner and organizer."

"Grandpa thinks its crazy but Mom is always meeting with people about it. Mr. Rueben comes by . . ."

"Who is Mr. Rueben?"

"I'm not really sure, he's moms friend, he . . . actually I think he's a detective now." She stops herself. "See daddy that is one of the things I don't understand. He comes by and talks to mom sometimes. Does that mean he's her boyfriend?"

"Not necessarily. He's a detective?" David replies nervously. "What do they talk about?"

"Stuff. He's been to dinner at our house a few times. They talk about mom's store, and they talk a lot about coffee. And you."

"What does he say about me?"

"Oh, I don't know. Stuff about how strange the accident was."

"What else does he say?"

"When they start talking about you, mom makes me go do my homework or chores or something. Why do you think he comes to see mom?"

"People need people around them sometimes; he doesn't want her to get lonely."

"But you are here."

"Yes and no. I guess it's like I was standing on the moon with no way of getting back. It would be mean of me to tell your mom to put her life on hold just in case I might get back."

"But you are here though."

"I've been thinking on this, I'm here but sort of not here. That probably doesn't make sense to you but that's what popped into my head. There are reasons I can't stay. I could get in a lot of trouble. But I do know its okay for me to be here now, at this time and place. It's safe for me to be here, to be with you."

"Is that why you only come now with everyone running around in costumes and you can dress up?"

"Maybe. Nobody is going to pay much attention to me. They will see what they think they should see, not much else."

He had thought about it but it is so strange, his existence seems to be wrapped around this one day, every year but it seems like everything, for him, folds into one day a year when he can safely see his daughter. He seems to be waving bye to Delta one Halloween eve then turn right around and there she is on the next Halloween. He desperately wants to find a way to see his daughter more often. Of course he couldn't tell her what his life was like or what he had become. Other than being her father, he wasn't sure himself anymore.

They continue to walk.

"Daddy, maybe you could go see lawyers or doctors or something. Maybe they can figure out how you can come home."

"I don't think they would be much help." He says smiling.

As they walk on, they hear a screeching sound behind them. A big blue sedan has jumped the curb and is headed for them and a bunch of other people on the sidewalk. Delta is frozen in place and her father has disappeared. Then everything seems to move as if underwater, moving slow and fluidly. She sees the hood of the car come toward her, inch by inch, the large chrome bumper will strike her first then she will fly up onto the hood. Delta can even see the horrified look of the young woman through the windshield. Perhaps five feet from Delta, the hood of the car begins to bend downward as if a huge weight has been put on it. The hood is deformed, bent in two spots as if two hands had pushed into the metal. The car stops and brushes into Deltas leg. The other people on the sidewalk scatter as the car comes to a stop. The woman inside the car is not so fortunate. She flies up into the windshield, hitting her head.

Delta looks in first to see a young woman slumped over the wheel, her head bleeding. Now everything is moving normally. David is now beside Delta staring through the windshield at the young woman in the car. Delta yells to her dad to help the woman. "Dad! Help her!"

David continues to stand there. The people that were on the sidewalk and other people outside begin to gather around. People begin to come out of their houses, first from the house nearest the accident, then from the ones next to it and so on. Scattered kids and adults trick or treating all gather around. Like tumbling dominoes, people open their doors to see what the fuss is about. Up and down the block, all the way to Delta's house and past, people are rushing over to the accident.

"Dad! Dad! Get her out of the car." Delta pleads with him. He reaches down to the car door and it falls from the hinges with the same effort it takes someone to open a soda and he lays the car door on the ground.

"Delta! Are you okay?" Delta turns away from the car; several people have rushed over.

"Dad, that was awesome. Did you stop the car? Of course you did. Man, you're like some kind of superhero!"

David grins slightly and shrugs. Then he looks over at the gathering crowd and tells them in a commanding voice, "This lady needs medical attention." All the people rush over to help as a siren wails. Someone has called the police and shortly a policeman arrives. Another siren wails, it's the ambulance.

"Come on Delta, time to make ourselves scarce." As Delta and David walk up the sidewalk, they catch snippets of the statements people are making to the arriving police.

"Did anyone see what happened?" The officer asks and people in the crowd start talking.

"He was 6 foot 4 with dreamy dark hair . . . I saw him when he ripped the door off." A woman in a house coat and curlers says.

"No, I saw the fella. I was out with my grand kids." And older man says. "Stopped the car from hitting some little girl. He had bulging muscles with arms like tree trunks . . ."

"Yeah man, he put his hands on the car hood and stopped it and then he tore the car door right off . . ." A teenager tells the officer.

"He did what?"

"I think he had a red cape . . ." A ten year old boy offers.

"I hate working on Halloween." The officer mutters.

As Delta and her dad walk briskly up the sidewalk toward Delta's house, they hear a voice, "Delta! Delta!"

David stops and back pedals toward the crowd. It's odd that none of the witnesses recognize him. Or maybe not, eye witnesses are not always reliable, particularly in such a quick, traumatic episode.

"Here, mom!"

"Are you okay?"

"Sure." She is a little dazed, the shock of almost getting run over. And her father has gone.

"Come on, honey, let's go home. This neighborhood just goes little nuts on Halloween." Seems like every year there's something going on." Her mother says. "What happened down there?" Doris motions to the accident.

Delta thinks a moment then says, "A car accident."

So they walk toward home.

"Mom."

"Yes."

"Mom, what happened to daddy?"

With a deep sigh, she begins the conversation she has long dreaded but tried to prepare herself for. Doris thinks the car accident probably prompted Delta to ask.

"Remember, honey, we talked about this, your daddy was in a car accident, like that car, except I'm sure everyone will be fine." She tries to end the covnerstation at that.

"No, I mean what happened. Tell me about it."

"Honey these things happen . . ."

"Did a dog run out in front of his car or something?"

"No." She wants to blurt out everything, just dump out everything. Somehow she keeps it in.

"So, something bad happened." Delta says rather than asks.

"Look its time for bed." She says floundering.

"No it isn't! Why won't you just tell me? I'm not a baby!" Delta says a little more petulantly than she intended.

"Do you really want to know?" Doris says in a quiet voice.

This causes Delta to hesitate before she says with as much conviction as she can manage. "Yes. I want to know."

"Let's get home and get to bed." Doris replies sullenly, not wanting to tell the words again, so that she herself has to hear what happened to her husband that Halloween night from years past.

"Mom, please. I gotta know." Delta reaches out for Doris but it is Doris who shrugs free and runs down the block toward their house.

Delta walks back to the house, trudges up the step and into the house. She comes into the living room, all the lights still on; Doris is sitting on the couch. Delta comes in and sits beside her. Waiting.

"It was an accident." Doris begins haltingly and with much effort. "He was in a horrible car accident. On Halloween. On his way home. There was no rush, he would have got home in plenty of time but he stopped off for beer with some of his work friends . . . there should have been plenty of time." Wistfully, she continues, "So many times I yelled at him for hanging out after work and drinking too much when he should have been home." Her face darkens, "But I guess I was upset about the wrong things. Maybe I was too much of a nag, maybe that's why he . . . Honey, sometimes people just have to relax, unwind so some people like to have a beer or something. I think your daddy was that way. He liked his drinking, you know, well not the drinking so much as hanging out with people. You know what I'm saying?"

Delta looks at her, sort of understanding.

"Your daddy liked stopping at this bar on the way home for a beer. That's why you have to be careful; you don't want to get intoxicated. I stood by and let your daddy go to that place." Doris shivers as she tells this to Delta. "So he stopped with his friends." Pausing, she spits out the rest of the story. "He had that woman in his car. Some woman he met in a bar. They were heading to . . ." Doris stops herself then continues. "His friends should have stopped him, he should have stopped himself, but he got in his car. He had too much to drink is what they said. He had a woman in the car that was what they said." She stops again, her eyes staring off.

Delta waits, she realizes there is more.

"Another car. Another car with a lady in it. She was drunk and hit your daddy's car." Doris stops, swallows with no tears in her eyes, and continues. "All of them died, himself, and he . . . and . . . and I guess there is nothing else to tell." Doris's voice breaking, trails off.

Delta was finally understanding with her maturing mind and not her child's heart, what had happened to her father. That, combined with nearly getting run over by a car, she begins to feel light headed. Delta collapses into her mother's arms.

Evening Seven

Detective Rueben was standing at the edge of a very large hole. The hole was rimmed with several bright flood lights directed down into the hole. Three men in gray jump suits were busy, carefully digging in the soggy dirt, the smell of gasoline so strong that the men had to climb out of the hole every fifteen minutes or so. Beside the detective was the gas station's ruptured fuel storage tank and on the other side of that was the new tank.

Earlier in the day, the old tank had been lifted from the hole. When some men climbed down into the pit to jackhammer out the old concrete pedestal that the fuel tank rested on, one of them spotted a hand or what was left it, half buried in the dirt.

It would be a few more hours until they could remove the body. Rueben was meticulous. He wanted to examine every bit of evidence himself. So when the techs from the morgue climbed out to take a break, Rueben climbed down the ladder. He stepped into wet but firm clay soil. He had his old tennis shoes and jeans on anticipating the mess. Even with the floodlights, he still needed his flashlight. He focused it on the area where the body was located. The beam traveled across the shadows, went past the body and he swung the beam back. He saw it. The hand still had some tissue attached. It was the left hand. And there was a wedding ring on the finger. A man's wedding ring.

Rueben walked over, squatted down and reached out to touch the hand. He knew who this was. He touched the ring. He could see how it all went down. Like watching a movie, Detective Rueben can see David in the bar. David is sipping on his beer as the owner of the bar; Wilbur talks to David.

"Kid, none of my business, but I'm going to stick my nose in anyway, I don't like this. Doesn't it strike you as kind of odd that a woman is trying to pick up guys in this bar? And she's a little too eager if you ask me, probably into some weirdness. That's messed up." Wilbur warns David.

"Come on." Lenny leans over toward David. "Don't you guys read Playboy? Women are into this sex stuff, you know, they're empowered."

"And don't you have to be home tonight to take your kid trick or treating." Wilbur tells David.

"You're right. I'll do a quick beer with her then I'm out the door." David says.

"See that you do." Wilbur tells him.

The blonde is sitting at her table drinking her martini, glancing over to make sure David is following her.

The man sitting alone and toward the back, gets up from his chair throws a few bucks on the table, leaving his newspaper, and heads for the door. He slowly walks toward the door, a little unsteady, glancing over at the blonde woman but all she gives him is a disapproving look. As he reaches the door, he misses the door handle as his hand is shaking just a bit.

"Hey buddy." Wilbur calls over to him. "Are you driving tonight?"

"What?"

"I said are you driving. You downed that last sour too fast. I'm going to need your keys."

"Ain't got no keys man, I'm not drivin."

Wilbur looks the guy over. "So where you headed?'

"I don't see how that's any of your business, dude."

Wilbur looks the kid over with the eye of a skilled soldier. "Makin it my business boy. You're not getting in your car or stumbling out of here."

The young man is not so drunk that he can't see that this older guy is not somebody to mess with.

Lenny interjects, "Look mister, he's just looking out for you."

"Fine. I'm staying at the hotel up the street." He replies as he opens the door and steps outside.

"Have a good evening." Wilbur says as the door closes and then under his breath, "Asswipe."

Things aren't usually this frisky around here." David says as he approaches the blonde woman.

"Took you long enough to get over here." She smiles up at him.

"I brought a peace offering.' He is holding another martini.

"Another one? Are you trying to get me smashed? I thought you were a nice guy." She pauses for a moment. "I'm glad I was wrong about that."

David begins to blush.

Giggling and pursing her red lips, "I am getting a bit thirsty." She says as she fingers her empty martini glass.

Sitting down, David puts the fresh martini glass on the table and slides it over to her; she makes sure her fingers touch his as she takes the glass. Underneath the table, she rubs her leg on his.

"Look, I didn't mean to lead you on but I do have to get home."

"Sure, you'll get home eventually." She smiles. "I just thought we could visit for a while David."

He frowns for a moment, "Have we met?"

"No."

"How did you know my name?"

She pauses. "Well, your buddies have been calling you that all night."

"Oh yeh, right. Well, you know my name . . . "

"I'm Jillian." She holds out her hand. He takes it and she holds it.

All Hallows Eve | 89

He realizes he has to get out of here. He is getting in over his head.

"Jillian, I do need to go. I gotta take my kid out for Halloween."

A frown slides across her face but she recovers quickly. "How about helping me finish the martini and you can walk me out to my car? Maybe I give you my phone number?"

"Jillian, I . . . "

"Tell you what, just help me finish up this martini and you can walk me out to my car." *She takes a sip from the glass and holds it to David's lips, he shrugs and he sips the rest. They slide back in their chairs and rise from the table. She slides her purse over one shoulder and slips on her jacket.*

As they head to the door, Wilbur gestures good night to David and Lenny says, grinning, "Don't do anything I wouldn't do!"

David waves sheepishly as he and Jillian slip out the door. As they walk along the sidewalk to the back parking lot, the downtown is deserted during mid week and particularly on a Halloween. She slips her right arm around his waist, he stumbles a little, walking hip to hip. David starts to pull away.

"Jillian, you're fantastic but seriously, I'm married." *He mumbles.*

"Just relax." *They make a left turn around the building and head down the alley to the back of the building.* "Is that your car?" *She points to one of three cars in the lot as they reach the back of the building. She feels a little dizzy. The drug she slipped into the martini was little more potent than she realized but this guy is still conscious. She thought he would be out by now. The drug has affected her and she begins to feel weak and light headed. She hangs on to David as he tries to pull away.*

Looking over David's shoulder, Jillian hisses, "Get over here and help me!"

Before David can say anything, a man steps up behind them and pulls David backward. David stumbles and falls backward. The silence is interrupted by a crunching sound as the back of his skull strikes the concrete curb. David's eyes are open and vacant. Jillian braces herself against the wall in the alley for a couple of minutes.

Bending over David, the man says, "I think he's dead, Jillian."

"What?" She replies groggily trying to clear her head. This wasn't supposed to happen.

"Yeh, he's dead." The man says getting up and prods David with the toe of his shoe. Jillian's entire body begins to shake, partly due to the drug and the shock of the dead man at her feet. The man just stares at the body, curious perhaps until Jillian regains her composure and she hisses to the scruffy, blonde haired man.

"Pick him up you idiot. We have to get out of here, drag him to his car." The scruffy man complies.

He drags David's body to the back of the car. She bends over, fishes keys out David's pocket. She fumbles through the keys to find the car key, and then opens the trunk. "Put him in before someone comes by, and then get his shirt off." The blonde guy takes off his jacket and lays it on the roof of the car then he lifts David into the trunk. He lifts the upper torso and then folds in the legs as David's head thumps on the side of the trunk. "I'll get his wallet and his work ID." Jillian says. The scruffy man then slams the trunk lid.

She goes around to the passenger side and opens the door and slides in. Her head is swimming but she forces herself to focus. She puts the key in the ignition and turns on the dome light. She pulls out a case from her purse. It contains a picture of the blonde guy, the same size as the photo on David's work badge. She tries to clear her head as she pastes the picture over David's picture and re-laminates the ID.

The man is buttoning up the shirt he took off David.

"Okay here's his badge and his wallet. I can't do anything to his driver's license but the picture's bad enough, I could pass for him." She cackles softly.

"Let's just get this done, Jillian."

"We have some time, but we need to be the first ones there for the early shift so you don't run into anybody that knows this guy and you can grab as much gold as you can."

"How do you know it's there?"

"How do I know? Cause I let that disgusting fat ass from the plant feel me up for the past month to find out how much gold they have, where it is and how to get it. This poor bastard is the only guy that gets to be alone with the gold because he's some artist or something and knows how to work with it."

"Isn't the gold going to be locked in a safe?"

The blood drains from her face as she realizes they needed to get the combination from David. "Damn it! Damn it!" She yells and pounds on the dashboard. They were going to get the combination from him while he was drugged. Her heart is pounding in her chest, maybe she is having a heart attack. No, she has to think. They need to get out of here. They need to get rid of the body. Maybe dump it out of town.

"We're getting out of here. Start the car."

"Where we going?"

"Anywhere. Just get on the road!"

"Okay, okay." He starts the car and turns off the dome light. The seat and mirrors are set perfectly. He backs out of the space, puts the car in drive and gets on the street that runs in front of the bank and the bar.

Suddenly Jillian yells for him to stop the car which he does. "There. Pull around to the back of the gas station. You can dump him in there." She gestures to the new gas station and the fuel tank in the big hole. The hole hadn't been fully back filled yet. And would be filled in first thing in the morning.

After dumping the body, they headed out of town toward their motel. They had left their car at the motel and caught a bus into town. The plan had been to drive David's car to the plant to steal the gold, leave a drugged out David at the motel and she would drive their car to the next town where they would rendezvous, and load up the gold. But all her planning went for nothing.

Now they would leave David's car at the motel and get as far from here as they could. And hope no one could identify them or find them. They arrived at the motel, it was getting late. They try to be as quiet as possible. They park beside their car.

"All right, you go in the room and grab our bags then get the car started. I'll wipe off the wheel, door handles, and trunk anything we touched in that guy's car." She opens the car door and uses a tissue to wipe of the interior and exterior door handles and closes the door quietly.

"Why aren't you in my car and where are the bags?" She asks the scruffy guy.

He glances down at the ground and shuffles his feet as he breathes out. "Well, the keys are in my jacket."

"And where is your jacket?"

"I took it off to lift this guy into the trunk. I must have left it on the car, it must have fallen off back in town."

She is livid but can't scream or else wake up the whole motel. "Get in the guy's car. I hope you didn't lose those keys."

"No, got em right here." He holds them over his head and jingles them.

"Get in the car." She mumbles via gritting teeth.

Moments later they are in the car and speeding down the highway. Jillian is huddled against the passenger door. She thought of all the greasy, pathetic men she had let touch her over the years. Starting with her stepfather. That's when she first learned that men would do things for her if she did certain things for them. All the men she had seduced including this idiot to get what she wanted. She thought it ironic that the only guy that didn't try to mess with her was the one that wound up dead.

The car headlights illuminate the pavement sliding underneath the car as they speed down the dark asphalt highway as the broken yellow lane lines create a relaxing and hypnotic rhythm. She begins to relax, the out of control events of the night begin to coalesce in her mind; what she had done and the inevitable results. She had planned to steal but not to hurt anyone. She just didn't want to be touched anymore. The more she thought about it, the more upset she became. She begins to cry. It's all unraveling. She thought if she could get enough money then . . . what? She really didn't know. She hadn't planned that far ahead.

The guy sees her crying out the corner of his eye. He reaches over, just to comfort her. When he touches her bare knee, she begins screaming at him.

She grabs her purse and pummels him with it. So hard that she breaks out the driver's side window. She hurls her purse at him and it flies out the window. Then she launches herself at him and scratches and hits him. The car begins to swerve across the center line. His foot reflexively presses the accelerator. Finally he shoves her off him and back across to the passenger side. He regains control of the car and gets on the right side of the road.

"Stop it you crazy bitch!" He yells at her. He glances over at her and looks into her face, a face twisted in a savage combination of rage, hurt and shame. They never see the headlights rushing toward them. Another car with a drunk driver that crosses the center line and plows into them. The head on impact launches him through the windshield and onto the pavement at 80 or 90 MPH, effectively skinning him alive. Jillian stays in the car as the engine block crashes thru the passenger compartment and pushes her crumpled body into the trunk.

Detective Rueben jerks his hand back. He's not quite sure what just happened but now he knows the truth. With this wedding ring, he can now prove it, at least most of it.

David felt something touch his hand. Warmth. He feels a sense of peace? No, more a feeling he would get after a challenging tennis game or a long jog. That sense of peace after finishing something difficult and then can rest for a little while until the next time, the next challenge. The warm touch distracted him momentarily as he waited for Delta. Would she come out for Halloween this year? He waited at the corner, as parents tried to corral their children while other children clung to their parents too afraid to ring a doorbell. Or older kids, teenagers or close to it, reluctantly escorting younger children from door to door. David felt strange this evening, so much so that he almost didn't see her. Didn't see her because she was no longer a little girl but a girl on her way to becoming a young woman. When he realized it was her, he felt a bit melancholy but also proud.

It is a sad/happy feeling that parents have about their children, particularly at night; after making sure their children have finished their homework, they've eaten their dinner including any green stuff, packed their lunches for school the next day, and brushed their teeth. After all this is done and parents have done their chores; cleaning the house, paying the bills, fixing the leaky faucet, calling a plumber to fix the faucet you tried to fix, and the hundreds of other tasks that people do everyday. Parents have one little task they do every night even when the dishes don't get washed or maybe you skip brushing your teeth but there is one thing you always do. Every night when the children are asleep, you peek into your kid's room to make sure they're okay. You're happy that your daughter is growing up but also sad that the little girl that laughs at all your lame jokes is slipping away from you. When they're teenagers, they lock the door but even then, you still stop by the door and even when they head off to college or get a job and move out, you still have the urge to stop by the door every night. Parenting is a full time job; you never quit and you never retire.

Delta is coming up the sidewalk toward him with a little girl in a princess costume. What is it with girls and princess costumes? She is holding the five year old girl's hand. It is a neighbor's child that Delta had agreed to baby-sit and take trick or treating since Delta was obviously too old for that kid stuff. The little girl stares at all the other kids running around. Then she sees David and starts laughing and pointing and says, "Look! Look! It's the king! The one from the story book, Delta." Delta had read her the *The Little Princess of Snow Lake*, the published version, not David's version.

Delta looks over at David and grins, "Yeah, I think you're right kid."

David looks down at his side and has a sword strapped to his waist which is very cool but he's wearing a long jersey that just barely covers his groin area and his buttocks. And he is wearing leather pants. He thinks to himself, 'Come on! This is a bit embarrassing. Why not a cool suit of armor?' Then he remembers the picture of the king from the book. He reaches up with his hand and touches his forehead and feels a metal crown of some sort. Wonderful.

The girl drops Delta's hand and runs up to David. "I'm the princess!"

David looks down at her and says, "You certainly are and a very good one."

"Sorry sir." Delta apologizes to him, she doesn't recognize him.

"That's okay." He considers telling her who he is but he realizes she wouldn't believe him. And somehow that is as it should be.

As they walk away, he can't resist. "Hey you two." Delta and the girl turn around. "I have a joke for you. What is a ghost's favorite dessert?" They look at him quizzically as he tells them the answer. "Ice Scream." The little girl giggles. As they turn to leave, David can tell by the tone of her voice and tilt of head that Delta is rolling her eyes as she says. "My dad used to tell silly jokes and stories too." At first David thinks that's some sort of an insultament, an insult with a trailing compliment. Or maybe it's a complisult, a compliment that ends as an insult. But Delta adds with a hint of sadness in her voice, "I miss his stories."

David smiles and tells her, "Take care." He watches over them as Delta and the little girl walk off into the night.

Edwards Brothers,Inc!
Thorofare, NJ 08086
19 January, 2011
BA2011019